DEATH ON PARADISE CREEK

BOOK ONE OF THE WILBARGER COUNTY
SERIES

DIANNE SMITHWICK-BRADEN

Paperback ISBN: 978-0-9992240-0-7
ebook ISBN: 978-0-9992240-1-4
Audio book ISBN: 978-0-999-2240-2-1

Published By DSB Mysteries
www.diannesmithwick-braden.com

Cover design by Dave King kingsize95@gmail.com

Printed in the United States of America
Suggested retail price $12.95

This book is dedicated to God. I know that without His help I would never have completed it. I also dedicate it to my husband, family, and friends whose help, support, and encouragement has been priceless.

DEATH ON PARADISE CREEK

ONE

It was going to be a beautiful spring day. There was a light breeze tickling the grass and the young leaves on the trees. The birds were singing their best notes to greet the morning sun as it gently warmed the earth.

Otis Turner was a creature of habit. He awoke each morning with the crow of the rooster. He rose immediately to shave and dress before breakfasting on two eggs, bacon, and coffee every morning at the café. He would then walk the short distance to work and remain there until noon when he would return to the café for his midday meal. In the evening, he would go to the saloon to have a small meal and discuss the events of the day and the advantages of statehood with other saloon patrons before going home to sleep. His routine never varied.

He dressed and breakfasted quickly that fine morning. He had a feeling that something big was about to happen. It was April 16, 1896. *Already one month since we became part of the Oklahoma territory,* he thought. *It's only a matter of time until Oklahoma will become a state.*

Otis was five feet five inches tall with an ample midsection. It had been several years since he had been able to see his shoes from a standing position. Only a rim of gray hair remained on his small round head. His bushy mustache still held traces of his former brown hair color. His skin was fair with pink undertones that became various shades of red depending on the level of his anger or excitement. He had small dark brown eyes that were continually shifting from side to side as if he expected to be attacked at any moment. His eyes stopped shifting on a few occasions. He would look someone in the eye when he was angry or when he was doing business. At those times his beady little eyes would focus directly on the person in question.

Otis never married because the most important thing in his life was business. His business was money, other people's money to be exact. Otis was the proprietor of the Bank of Willow. He took great pleasure in counting the money in the bank safe each evening after closing and each morning before opening. He knew at any given moment exactly how much money was in his bank because he kept a running total in his mind of each transaction. He felt as if each dollar and coin were his personal possessions. Customers making deposits were always welcomed with open arms. He seemed to be offended when a customer made a withdrawal or asked for a loan. He often bragged that his bank was as robbery proof as it could possibly be.

Otis valued only one thing as much as money and that was his reputation. He believed himself to be the most respected and powerful man in town as well as the most desired by the ladies. He became quite angry if anyone contradicted him or failed to listen to one of his endless lectures about the money to be made when statehood was achieved.

The truth was that no one took Otis very seriously. The townspeople thought he was full of hot air but took good care of their money. The ladies in town seldom gave him a second thought. Some of the ranch hands had great fun making him angry just to see him turn red and hear him sputter. They had no idea that he hoped one day to be mayor of Willow.

Willow was a small community in the southwestern part of the Oklahoma territory. It had the establishments necessary to sustain a community of one hundred fifty citizens including the bank, general store, café, and saloon. It was a quiet little town most of the time. It became livelier when pay day rolled around for the ranch hands. Then the nearby ranchers, farmers, and their hands came into town for supplies and socializing.

Three of the men that rode into Willow that spring afternoon were Frank, Harold, and Joseph Keys. Until that morning, they had worked for one of the local ranchers. Over the course of the past year they had worked for every ranch in the area. Frank and Harold had been fired again. Joseph quit out of loyalty to his brothers.

Frank and Harold were identical twins. At twenty-two years old, they were big, burly, handsome men with curly auburn hair, mischievous gray eyes, and disarming grins. At six feet three inches tall and two hundred twenty-five pounds each of solid muscle, they were definitely an intimidating sight. The only way to distinguish between the pair was that Harold had a small scar below his right eye where he had been cut in a brawl.

The pair seemed to be magnets for trouble from the time they could walk. Trouble found them even when they were trying to stay on the straight and narrow. They were good natured most of the time but had tempers that would flare in an instant and subside just as quickly. They never backed down from a fight, real or imagined. They would always see the error of their ways after the fact and took the consequences for their actions in stride. Fortunately, they had not broken any laws or done any real harm.

The men of Willow liked the twins and knew there were no better fights to watch when they were in a temper. The women of Willow found them very attractive and just dangerous enough to be interesting.

If Frank and Harold had a weakness, it was their eighteen year old brother Joseph. They bossed him around because he was the youngest, but they did everything in their power to protect him.

Ida, their mother, had died shortly after Joseph was born. Their father, Jeb, promised her that all of the boys would go to school. He kept his word until Frank and Harold's natural ability for getting into trouble resulted in their being kicked out of school. He put them to work on the family farm. He taught them about farm and ranch work, and how to hand tool leather.

While all three boys learned the skills their father possessed, Joseph stayed in school learning the skills his brothers never did. The four men worked the family farm often losing more money than they made. Joseph kept a journal of the income and expenses. He would also record things that he wanted to remember. He continued to keep the journal after their father passed away. The three boys sold the farm and took jobs with a local rancher.

Joseph was a slightly smaller version of his brothers. He weighed one hundred seventy-five pounds at six feet tall. His hair was auburn like his brothers but not as curly. His gray eyes and his ready smile held warmth and laughter. He too was all muscle from hard ranch work.

People were drawn to Joseph. His good humor was in sharp contrast to the quick tempers and iron fists of his siblings. Joseph could hold his own in a fight but seldom did if a fight could be avoided.

There were other differences, too. The twins acted first and thought about it later. Joseph thought everything through. He would look at a situation from every angle before making a decision to act.

Since the twins were most often the center of attention for one reason or another, Joseph was able to stay in the background and observe. Joseph learned a lot about people by watching their interactions with each other and reactions to his brothers. He could read people and anticipate their actions. This ability was especially helpful where his brothers were concerned.

He would recognize the signs when their employers or fellow ranch hands were growing tired of his brothers' antics. He would pack up the hand tooled saddlebags their father had made with their belongings and what money they had in preparation for a hasty departure.

The saddlebags were their prized possessions. Each one bore the initials of its owner along with an image of five keys on a ring, one key to represent each member of the family. They were reminders of the home and family they once had.

Joseph loved his brothers dearly. They were the only family he had. He did all he could to protect them and he knew they would do anything to protect him.

As they rode into Willow, the Keys boys were discussing where they should go to find work. They had decided to stay the night in town and ask around to see if anyone would hire them. Each dreaded the thought of leaving the area and looking for work elsewhere. They decided to split up and meet later at the saloon.

Joseph went to the general store and bought a few supplies while making conversation with Mr. Cherry, the owner. Mr. Cherry knew of one ranch that was hiring. Joseph was hopeful until he heard it was the Adams ranch. They had been fired from that one three months earlier. He made his way to the bank where he learned that he would be welcome to work at any of the ranches but without his brothers.

Frank had gone to the blacksmith and livery stable while Harold had gone to the café and hotel. They had learned the same information that Joseph had learned. Dejected, they went to the saloon to wait for Joseph.

The sun was low on the horizon when Joseph met his brothers at the saloon. They discussed their situation and decided to ride out to their home place the next morning for one last look before leaving Willow to look for work elsewhere.

They found a table and ordered a meal. They ate greedily, not knowing when they would get a chance to eat well again.

Otis Turner was in a corner of the saloon lecturing again about the benefits of statehood. He didn't notice that only one man was really listening to him until he mentioned that he felt he was the only logical choice for mayor of Willow. No one cheered. *Maybe if he said it louder.*

"I am the best and only logical choice for mayor," he boasted.

The patrons in the saloon were stunned into silence.

That's more like it, he thought. *Now I have their undivided attention.* Rather than the applause and cheers he expected, laughter rang in his ears. Otis fastened his gaze on each man in turn. He became redder as the laughter became louder. He stormed out of the saloon crimson faced with all the dignity he could muster. He took refuge in his bank and found comfort by counting the money in the safe.

A poker game began shortly after Otis departed and the laughter subsided. Frank and Harold joined in while Joseph went to the hotel to reserve a room for the night. He then went to visit Alice Jeffries, a local young woman he had been seeing.

It had been hard telling Alice goodbye. He wandered around town thinking about their conversation.

"We're going to leave Willow tomorrow to look for work," he told her. "I don't know when or if we'll be back this way."

She cried as she pointed out that he didn't have to leave. "You can get a job anywhere around here. You can stay and let your brothers go on without you."

"I'll think about it Alice," he said as he left her crying.

He knew she was right. He was thinking about that conversation as he passed the saloon. He heard Frank's familiar laugh. He looked in and watched as Frank raked in the pot from the hand he had just won. No, he wouldn't stay. He'd go with them. They were all he had. Having made that decision, he went to the hotel to sleep.

Frank and Harold had been taking turns winning at the poker

table. They had never had such luck. One by one the players left the table until only the twins and one other man remained. The man was a stranger in town and had lost the last three hands.

"I'm just passing through and needed some relaxation before turning in for the night. Poker is my kind of relaxation."

He smiled at the twins as he continued, "Boys, I'm getting mighty sleepy, but I hate to leave a game so evenly matched. What do you say to one more hand, winner take all?"

Frank and Harold had been winning most of the night and thought they couldn't lose. They winked at each other, grinned, and said in unison, "Sounds like a fine idea."

Fifteen minutes later, they were leaving the saloon completely broke. They had not only lost all of their winnings but all of their pay as well. The stranger said, "Goodnight." He chuckled as he passed the twins outside the saloon. At that moment, they realized they had been cheated. They looked at each other and at the same instant decided to follow the man.

The man heard footsteps behind him. He turned to see two identical angry faces. He started to run down the street. He ran past the bank and turned into the alley beside it. He could see a light in a window and knocked frantically on the door next to it.

Otis Turner peered cautiously out the door and asked, "What do you want?" His eyes darted from side to side.

"I need to make a deposit quick," the stranger replied.

"Well, it's after hours, but since I'm here come on in." Otis opened the door for the stranger. The transaction was made and the stranger cautiously left the bank.

The stranger saw Frank and Harold waiting at the end of the alley for him to come back. There was no other way out.

He walked toward them and said nervously, "It's no use boys. I've just deposited every nickel in the bank. You won't gain anything by harming me."

Frank growled, "All we want is our pay back. You can keep the rest."

The man trembled and said, "I won it fair and square."

Harold glared at him and snarled, "I don't think so, mister."

The man yelped and ran down the street. The twins knew the money was in the bank, so they didn't bother to follow him.

"Maybe the banker will give us our pay if we explain the situation," Harold said hopefully.

"Maybe," Frank answered. "Wonder if he'll talk to us now or if we'll have to wait till morning?"

The light was still on in the bank. They made their way to the back door. It was ajar. They could see a stack of money on the table. Otis had his back to them putting money in the safe.

All they wanted was their wages. They looked at each other and nodded. They were only going to reach in, get their money, and leave; hopefully without being seen. They covered their faces with the bandanas they wore around their necks and pulled their hats down low just to be safe.

They gently and slowly pushed the door open. When it was wide enough for one of them to slip through, the door creaked. The twins froze. Otis whirled around to find the two large masked men in the doorway.

His face turned crimson as Otis realized what was happening. He reached for his gun, but the men were too quick for him. Frank grabbed the gun and tossed it aside while Harold wrapped his arm around Otis and forced him to the floor. Finding some twine used to tie money bags, Frank tied the banker's hands and feet. Otis turned maroon when Harold gagged him with his own handkerchief. Otis was lying on the floor with his back to the door but facing the safe.

"We're sure sorry, Mr. Banker. That stranger cheated us. All we want is our pay. We'll leave the rest." Frank said.

Otis watched helplessly as the two men counted out their money. He was trying his best to find some feature that he recognized. As the two men headed for the door, one of them put the remainder of the money in the safe and locked it. The other blew out the lamp. They quietly closed the bank door behind them as they left.

The twins were feeling pretty good about themselves as they made their way to the hotel. Slowly they began to realize they had just robbed a bank. By the time they reached the hotel and got to their room, they had decided to leave town right away.

"You did what?" Joseph said in astonishment when his brothers told him of the evenings events. He was stunned. His brothers had never broken the law before. At least no one was hurt. Maybe they could still set things straight.

The three discussed a number of options until they finally agreed on a plan. Frank and Harold gave Joseph the money they had taken from the bank. They gathered up their gear and rode out of town toward their old home place to the west then turned back toward a playa lake a few miles east of town.

Joseph took the money and made his way to the bank. When he reached the alley, he took the precaution of covering his face and pulling his hat low. He didn't want the banker to recognize him and figure out who had taken the money.

Joseph started toward the door and noticed a light in the window. *They said they blew that out*, he thought. He tiptoed a little closer. The door was still closed. He peered inside. The safe was open and empty. There was no banker, only some twine, and a handkerchief lying on the floor.

TWO

As soon as the Keys twins had closed the door, Otis began struggling to free himself from his bonds. In his rage, he wanted revenge. His mind was racing. *How dare they do this to me! They'll pay for this! I'll be a laughing stock when every one finds out how little was taken and how easily!* Otis fumed. *Who were they? They were familiar but who were they? The man who made the deposit! He must know who they were. He must have seen their faces.*

As the thought of catching the thieves ran through his mind, Otis freed one hand from his bonds. It took only a minute more to gain his freedom. He struggled to his feet, lit the lamp, and went to the safe. They *took so little. I can hardly tell any is missing,* he thought, and an idea began to form. *No one else knows how much was taken. Of course, the thieves know, but who is going to believe a couple of bank robbers?* He rubbed his hands together at his own genius.

He cleaned out the safe putting the money in nearby money bags. He hid the bags under his desk beneath some loose floor boards. He planned to move it to his house a little at a time later. He replaced the floor boards and stood up. Now, it was time to find the sheriff.

Joseph saw movement out of the corner of his eye and stepped back as the banker rose from under his desk. Joseph hid in the shadows and watched the plump arrogant little man close the door and make his way down the alley whistling as he went.

Something isn't right, Joseph thought. *Why was the banker under the desk? The twins said they left him in front of the safe.*

Joseph quietly went into the bank and looked around. The twine and handkerchief were in front of the safe. *Why was he under the desk?* Joseph wondered. He walked around to the desk and looked under it. He couldn't see anything obvious.

The banker must have been on his hands and knees, or I would have seen him when I looked through the window. He knelt down and felt under the desk. He found a loose floor board and pried it up. He was furious. That pompous wind bag was going to let his brothers take the blame while he got away with the money.

For the first time in his life, Joseph acted without thinking things through. He took the bags of money and hid them under an old tub in the alley. If Frank and Harold were going to be arrested, he'd take the money, and they'd run for Mexico. If not, he'd leave the money where it was for a while just to see Otis squirm. He went back to the hotel to wait.

Joseph could see the main street pretty well from his window. He saw Otis and the sheriff walk across the street to the hotel. He got into bed and rumpled the blankets to give the appearance of having been asleep should the sheriff come calling. He lay there listening intently. He heard footsteps on the stairs and in the hall. They passed his door. Maybe they didn't suspect his brothers. He heard a knock on a door somewhere down the hall. He crept out of bed to the door trying to hear the conversation.

"It's Sheriff Blake. Please, open the door. I need to speak with you."

"What? Why? What's wrong? I didn't do anything."

"Otis, is this the man?"

"Yes, it is."

"What? Wait I didn't do anything! Hey, aren't you the banker?"

"Yes, I'm Otis Turner."

"What's the problem?"

"Mister?" the sheriff asked.

"Tate. Ernest Tate"

"Well Mr. Tate, I understand you were playing poker in the saloon this evening."

"Yes, I was," Tate replied warily.

"Do you know the men you were playing with?"

"There were several. What's going on?"

"Why were you in such a hurry to deposit your money? Couldn't it have waited until morning?"asked Blake.

"N...n...no, I was afraid. Are you going to tell me what this is all about?"

"After I've found out what I want to know. Why were you afraid?"

"Two of the men thought I had cheated them. I won it fair and square, Sheriff. I swear! They followed me out of the saloon. I was afraid they were going to steal my money and kill me. When I saw the light on in the bank, I thought it would be a safe place to hide. Then this man was there," pointing at Otis, "so I decided to deposit the money. They couldn't take it from me if it was safe in the bank."

"Who were they?"asked the sheriff.

"I...I didn't catch their names."

"Can you describe them?"

"Big guys, curly hair, looked just alike. Didn't know which was which?"

"Frank and Harold Keys? Do you think it could have been them Otis?"

"I didn't see their faces, but there was something familiar about them. The men said the stranger had cheated them, and they wanted their money. They were about the right size to have been Frank and Harold."

Joseph felt ill as he crept back to his bed. He waited for the sheriff to come looking for Frank and Harold.

He heard the men pass his door and descend the stairs. He could hear muffled conversation below but couldn't understand what was being said. Again he heard someone coming up the stairs. The footsteps grew louder as they moved down the hallway. They stopped at his door. He heard a pistol being cocked.

He tried to stay calm and relaxed. He wanted the men at the door to believe he had been sleeping soundly. He heard a key turn in the lock and the door creak as it slowly opened. *Don't move*, he thought. He felt a boot kick the bed. He didn't move until he felt a hand on his shoulder shaking him.

"Huh? What?" Joseph mumbled as he sat up.

"Be real still there, mister."

"Who is it? What do you want?"

"This one's Joseph. It's Sheriff Blake. Where are your brothers?"

"Why? What's wrong?"

"Well, these two gentlemen here believe they robbed the bank tonight."

"What! Sheriff, you know they'd never do a thing like that."

"I know they've never broken any laws before, but this man here," pointing at Tate "gave a real good description of them."

"You mean you saw them rob the bank?" Joseph was getting concerned now. The twins said no one had seen them.

"No, I didn't see them, but they were following me when I made the deposit."

"Did anyone see the bank robbers?" Joseph asked

"I did! I saw them with my own two eyes!" Otis's face was approaching maroon again as he recalled being bound and gagged.

"You saw Frank and Harold?"

"Well no, not exactly. I couldn't see their faces. They wore bandanas. But the description Mr. Tate gave matches their size and build."

"So you don't know for a fact that it was my brothers, only that it might have been them," Joseph said frowning at the banker.

Otis looked at Joseph with defiance and rage. Mr. Tate looked away sheepishly.

"Did you cheat them, Mr. Tate?"

"Of course not! Poker is a little relaxing pastime of mine. Sometimes I get lucky." No one in the room was convinced.

"I need to ask them some questions. Where are they Joseph?"

"I don't know. The saloon I guess. That's where I saw them last."

"When was that?"

"I'm not sure. We ate. I went to see a friend. They were still there playing poker when I passed the saloon on the way here."

"Who is this friend?"

"Why? Am I a suspect too?"

"I just wanted to get an idea of the time. You haven't been accused of anything."

"If you must know, I went to call on Alice Jeffries."

The sheriff raised an eye brow, "Alice Jeffries?"

"Yes, sir!"

"All right, if you see or hear from your brothers, tell them I need to speak with them."

"I'll do that. Are you looking for anyone else, Sheriff?"

"I'm taking a serious look at anyone who fits Mr. Turner's description. Goodnight, Joseph."

"Goodnight, Sheriff."

The three men left Joseph to contemplate what he should do now. *Chances are the sheriff is going to be keeping an eye on me. I'll just act the concerned brother until I see which way the wind blows,* he thought.

He slept fitfully the rest of the night. He heard footsteps and knocks on doors. He wasn't sure if the sounds were real or imagined.

The next morning, Joseph went to see the sheriff. He needed to find out what was happening.

"Mornin' Sheriff. Have you heard anything about the bank robbers?"

"Nothin' new. Any word from your brothers?"

"No, they didn't come back last night. I'm getting a little worried. It isn't like them to just leave."

"This whole mess is out of character for those two. I don't know what to make of it."

"Do you think Mr. Tate is telling the truth?"

"There's no doubt that Tate is a shady character. If he was involved in the robbery, he had partners."

"So it's possible that he may have set the whole thing up. Do you think he might have killed Frank and Harold so he could lay the blame on them?"

"I suppose it's possible, but I can't imagine that little guy getting the drop on both of them. Whoever it was that robbed the bank, it was not Mr. Tate. He doesn't fit the description that Otis Turner gave."

"I need to tell you something, Sheriff. You'll find out anyway if you haven't already. We were fired yesterday. Our pay was all we had to make a fresh start somewhere new. I'm sure Frank and Harold were trying to make some extra cash at the poker table. The trouble is that they hardly ever win. They always keep some back just in case. It's just not like them to rob a bank."

"I don't plan to arrest your brothers for something they didn't do. They are the only suspects so far that fit the banker's description. I promise you that I'll find the truth before I arrest anyone."

"That's fair enough."

Joseph walked out of the sheriff's office deep in thought. It was obvious to him that the only possible suspects were his brothers. There wasn't much time before a posse would be formed. He walked to the general store and bought a few supplies, and new saddlebags.

He told Mr. Cherry that his saddlebags had finally worn out. Mr. Cherry knew that the Keys boys would never part with the saddlebags their father had made any other way. He talked with Mr. Cherry until he saw Otis go into the café.

As he left the general store, he wondered if the banker had discovered that the money was no longer in the bank. Otis couldn't tell anyone since it was supposed to have been stolen in the robbery. Joseph smiled as he imagined the look on the bankers face when he made the discovery.

It serves him right, Joseph thought. *I could tell the sheriff what I saw, but then, I'd have to admit that Frank and Harold had robbed the bank.*

Going down the alley and locating the tub, Joseph filled the new saddlebags with the money from the bank. Now, he was the real bank robber, and no one suspected it.

Joseph didn't think anyone was watching him since he had managed to gather the money without attracting anyone's notice. He went about his day playing the part of the worried brother. He asked about his brothers at every business. He asked around the saloon for details of the poker game. He checked in with the sheriff again that evening before returning to his hotel room. There were no other possible suspects in town that matched the description given by Otis Turner.

Joseph went through the motions of going to bed that night. In reality, he was waiting for the right time to slip out of town to meet his brothers. He crept out of his room when the clock downstairs struck one. He made his way to the livery stable, saddled his horse, and quietly walked to the edge of town. He walked his horse until he could see lights in the distance behind him. When he felt he was safely away, he got on his horse and rode to the playa lake where his brothers waited.

Frank and Harold had been taking turns keeping watch. At the sound of the approaching rider, they took cover with their guns ready.

Joseph called out to them as he slowly grew near. They relaxed and came out to greet him.

After pouring himself a cup of coffee, Joseph told them what had been happening in town. He told about how Otis had set them up and how he had taken the money from Otis. The twins were astounded when Joseph handed them the saddlebags containing the cash.

"I expect a posse will be forming real soon, probably in the morning. What are we going to do?"

Frank and Harold looked at each other and back at Joseph.

"We're going south. You're going back to town."

"What? No! You can't be serious! I want to go with you!"

"Now just listen a minute," replied Harold. "We'll lay a false trail that will keep the posse real busy. We'll head south after that. You'll go back to town to keep an eye on what's happening. When the posse leaves, you'll head south to meet us. We'll have an idea of how far behind the posse is, and they won't be looking for you. If they discover you've left town, the posse will form for sure, and they'll be looking for you along with us."

Joseph was silent for several minutes before he reluctantly replied, "Where am I supposed to meet you? I've never been anywhere without you two."

"Do you remember that little place south of here in Texas that Pa used to talk about?" Frank asked. "He always told us just how to get there from the home place."

"Paradise something?"

"Paradise Creek. That's where he used to take Ma for picnics when they were courtin'. We'll meet you at that big ole pecan tree he always talked about."

"All right, but I'd rather go with you now."

"This is the best way believe me," Frank replied.

Joseph sighed and said, "Guess I better get back then. It'll be daybreak soon."

The brothers shook hands. As Frank and Harold watched Joseph ride away, they looked at each other and shook their heads. Chances were the posse would find them before Joseph would. At least he would be safe and free of suspicion. They broke camp and began laying the false trail for the posse to follow. They would sleep if they reached Paradise Creek.

THREE

Joseph had crept back into town and his hotel room unobserved. He went back to bed and slept soundly until a noise in the hallway woke him. He decided to continue playing the part of the worried brother. After he had dressed, he went directly to the sheriff's office.

"Hello, Sheriff. Any news?"

"No, afraid not. Any word from your brothers?"

"No, sir. This just isn't like them."

"I know it isn't but..."

"Sheriff, Sheriff!"

"What is it Otis?"

"What are you doing to catch the bank robbers?"

"Calm down Otis. Why are you in such an all fired hurry all of the sudden?"

The red in his face deepened as he spluttered, "It's been a whole day since the robbery. The trail will be getting cold if you don't do something right away."

"Otis the trail isn't any harder to follow than it was to begin with. It's hard to find a bank robber when you don't know who it is or where he is likely to go."

"He knows. I'm sure he knows. Why aren't you questioning him?" Otis glared at Joseph.

"Otis, Joseph has been in here at least three times for news. Now do you really think that he would do that if he knew where his brothers were?"

Otis spluttered, whirled around, and left the two men staring after him. Sheriff Blake shook his head and grinned. Joseph grinned back before strolling out of the sheriff's office and down the street. *I bet old Otis discovered that his stash is missing*, Joseph laughed to himself. *I had better keep an eye on him.*

Otis seemed to have the same idea about Joseph. Everywhere Joseph went that day, Otis wasn't far behind. His normal tidy attire was rumpled and dirty. People noticed his appearance and change of routine. When Otis finally gave up and returned to his bank, Joseph returned to his hotel room.

Each day it was the same. Joseph would start his day at the sheriff's office, keep an eye on Otis, let Otis keep an eye on him, and return to the hotel in the evening. The sheriff was under pressure to do something from Otis and the people of Willow. The life savings of most of the people had been taken.

Six days after the robbery, Sheriff Blake rode to a neighboring town following a lead in his investigation. Otis took the opportunity to form a posse. The leader of the posse was Clay Adams, a local rancher who had lost everything in the robbery. If the money wasn't recovered, he wouldn't be able to pay his hands. They would leave to find jobs that paid. Adams was the kind of man who acted impulsively and then thought about what he had done afterward with little or no regret. He soothed his conscience by laying the blame on someone or something else.

Joseph watched the posse form from his hotel window. He knew his brothers had a good head start on them, but he wasn't sure if the posse would follow the false trail. The posse rode out of town toward their old home place. Joseph let the dust settle before leaving his room. He made sure that he was seen at some of the local establishments before saddling his horse and leaving Willow. He felt a mixture of sadness to be leaving the only place he had ever called home and excitement for the adventure he was about to begin.

He headed northwest to mislead anyone who might be watching him. He could lead folks on a wild goose chase as well as his brothers when necessary. He didn't think anyone was paying attention to his movements, but he didn't want to take the chance.

Sheriff Blake hadn't gone to follow a lead. Instead, he sat on a ridge that overlooked the town. He observed all who entered and left Willow. He saw the posse ride west toward the Keys home place. He had already been there and found no sign of the twins or anyone else. He saw a lone rider traveling northwest. *The boy was right. It wasn't like his brothers to leave him behind. Not like them at all.* He was pretty sure the boy had an idea if not actual knowledge of where his brothers were hiding. All he had to do was to wait for Joseph to lead him to them. It looked like his waiting was about to pay off.

Joseph made his way northwest until midday. He stopped to let his horse rest and ate a small meal of biscuits. He would have a short nap and then start south.

Sheriff Blake had been tracking Joseph since he left Willow. He could see the horse grazing in the distance. He assumed that Joseph was letting his horse rest. He took the opportunity to let his own horse rest.

Joseph was in that place between sleep and wakefulness when he heard it. *Was that a horse? It was too far away to be mine,* he thought. He was fully awake now but lay very still listening. He thought that maybe he had been dreaming until he heard the sound again. It could be someone traveling the same way or someone could be following him.

There was a hill in the distance. He would be able to see if anyone was trailing him from the top. He rode for half an hour to the bottom of the hill. He looked back but couldn't see anyone. He continued to the top of the hill and turned. A lone rider appeared to be tracking him. He didn't know who the man was, and he didn't plan to stick around to find out. He went down the far side of the hill sweeping the tracks as he went. He then laid a false trail leading to the north and another to the west before traveling south and sweeping his tracks behind him. He hoped he had done enough to confuse the rider, but he wasted no time leaving the hill behind.

Blake reached the bottom of the hill and looked up. Obvious tracks leading to the top. *He isn't trying to hide anything*, he thought. The sheriff followed the tracks to the top of the hill.

No tracks going down. "Well, it's certain he didn't fly off this hill," he said to his horse. The sheriff got off his horse and began to search the ground more carefully. He found the false trails that Joseph had left. He continued to search but found no other trail.

"Okay, boy. Which one is the real trail?" Sheriff Blake asked his horse. The horse blinked but didn't offer an opinion. "Well, I guess we'll try this one first." He got back in the saddle and followed the northern trail.

Joseph wondered if the posse had followed the false trail his brothers had made. He rode south four days. During that time, he crossed the Red River and the Pease River. He knew that he should be getting close. He was tired and hungry. Thinking he might have gone the wrong way, he stopped to survey his surroundings. He was trying to remember the story his father had told them when he saw a big tree in the distance. He got off his horse and walked slowly to the tree. Harold lay sleeping in the shade. He looked around the area for Frank when suddenly he found himself lying on his back looking up at the sky.

"How's that for a welcome brother?" Harold had not been sleeping after all and had yanked Joseph's feet from under him. Joseph grinned at him after he caught his breath.

"Where's Frank?"

"It's his turn to get supper. I expect he'll be here shortly."

Frank returned with several fresh rabbits to roast over the campfire. The three men ate as Joseph told them all that had happened in Willow. The twins didn't have much to tell since they had seen no other human on their journey.

"We buried the money in the creek bank for safe keeping. If anyone tries to rob us or if the posse should show up, they won't find any money on us. Maybe they'll decide to go on their way and leave us be," Harold told him.

Frank promised to show Joseph where the money was buried after they had finished eating. They agreed that it would be a good idea to move on as soon as Joseph had rested. His horse needed rest too.

They camped for the night at the base of the pecan tree where their parents had picnicked near the bank of Paradise creek. They could hear the water trickling in the creek from their camp.

Joseph woke first the next morning. He decided he'd let his brothers sleep and go hunting for their breakfast. They were better hunters, but he wanted to see what he could find. It wouldn't hurt to have a good meal before moving on. He saddled his horse and rode away from camp. A short distance away he spotted a deer. Tempting as it was, he knew they couldn't use that much meat right now. He tied his horse to a mesquite tree and walked a hundred yards farther when a pheasant flew up practically in his face. His reaction was to protect his face and head causing him to drop his rifle. As his heart slowed, he cursed himself and picked up his weapon.

Joseph noticed something in the brush. He moved a little closer for a better look. It was the pheasant nest filled with eggs. *That wasn't so bad after all. I saved ammunition and got breakfast too,* Joseph thought.

He gathered the eggs, cradled them in his hat and went back to his horse. He rode back to camp quite pleased with himself.

Joseph reached the creek and followed it back to camp. He could hear raised voices and slowed down. He could see Frank and Harold.

They were on their horses, but their hands were behind their backs. Joseph got off his horse and took cover among the mesquites and the brush along the edge of the creek. He couldn't see very well, but he knew there were other men at the camp. He crept closer. It was the posse! Clay Adams was stirring them up saying, "Hang 'em! Hang 'em!"

Joseph's heart was in his throat. He started to leave his hiding place when he caught Frank's eye. He shook his head slightly. Harold saw him too and shook his head. They wanted him to stay where he was. They were trying to protect him, and there was nothing he could do to protect them.

A noose was slipped over Frank's head. Joseph couldn't breathe. He watched as a second noose was slipped over Harold's head. He tried to think of something he could do to help them.

"Clay, don't you think we should see if they have the money before we think about hangin' anybody?"

"They have it all right. It's just a matter of findin' it."

Clay meant to scare the brothers so that they would tell them where the money was hidden. Then they would hang.

"The only money we have is what there is left of our pay. It's right there in our saddlebags."

"Where's the money you stole from the bank?"

"We didn't steal any money from any bank?"

"You lie!"

The shouting made the twins' horses nervous. One of the posse members was emptying the saddlebags making noise and frightening the horses all the more.

Joseph watched in horror as one of the men stepped on a large stick. It cracked like gunfire. The frightened horses reared. They knocked down the men that were holding them and ran leaving Frank and Harold hanging from the big tree. Joseph couldn't move. He couldn't breathe. Tears filled his eyes. He watched as if in a dream as his brothers swayed in the air.

The men of the posse were silent for a moment.

"What do we do now?"

"Clay?"

"Search the camp. The money has to be here somewhere."

"What do we do with them?"

"Leave 'em."

Joseph somehow found the strength to move away from the creek and led his horse to a cluster of trees. There he waited for the posse to leave. He sat numb for hours listening to the men search. Each curse and shout told him that they had not found the buried money.

Clouds were building in the west. Thunder rumbled, lightening flashed, and the wind began to blow. The posse decided to give up with the coming storm. They saddled up and rode to the nearby town of Vernon. Joseph stayed in his shelter and waited for the storm to end. He was not going to leave his brothers.

Joseph was scared. He wanted to bury his brothers. What would he do if the posse came back? He decided to leave the money hidden until his brothers were buried. Where should he bury them? Would the posse accuse him if they came back and found him?

He decided to bury Frank and Harold on the opposite side of the creek among some mesquites and junipers. If the posse came back, it would be harder to find. He crossed the creek and found a place to dig. With tears in his eyes, he dug one large grave.

They were together from birth till death, he thought. *They should be together in the afterlife.*

After resting for a long while, he crept back across the creek to the big tree. There was no sign of the posse. He led his horse under the tree so that Harold would fall across the saddle. He cried as he cut his brother down and struggled to position Harold onto his horse. He took him across the creek to the grave and then went back to repeat the process with Frank. He laid them side by side with their saddlebags on their chests. He considered burying the money with them but decided that the posse might find the grave and the money. That thought made him feel as if his brothers had died in vain.

Joseph had almost finished burying his brothers when he heard horses. Terrified, he quietly made his way to the brush along the bank so that he could see the camp without being seen.

What will they do when they discover Frank and Harold are gone? He wondered as fear gripped his heart. He froze where he was just as he had before. There were two horses, but he could see no men. One of the horses turned enough that he recognized it. She was Frank's horse. The other horse was Harold's. He went into the camp, gathered up what was left of their belongings, and led the horses across the creek to the grave. Joseph spent the night there exhausted and grieving.

No one in the posse spoke during the ride to Vernon. Most were disturbed by the lynching. Adams was still searching Paradise Creek in his mind. He had no doubt that the money was there. He was angry that the boys died before he could find out where they had hidden it.

The posse rode into Vernon tired, hungry, and thirsty. They found the saloon where they ordered drinks and a meal. It wasn't long before the whisky had loosened their tongues. Adams told anyone who would listen that money was buried somewhere along Paradise Creek that belonged to the town of Willow.

They were out of supplies. Their ranches had been neglected for a week. The next morning they began the journey back to the Oklahoma Territory.

Joseph woke with a start the next morning. It hadn't been a dream. The nightmare had been real. Joseph had never known such fear.

He took a few deep breaths and contemplated his situation. He couldn't report what had happened without admitting that he had been there too. *Would they hang him? If he returned the money, would they still hang him? Maybe he should go to Mexico as planned.*

What would happen if the posse followed him? If they didn't, what would happen if someone discovered he had so much money?

After pondering for more than an hour, he made a decision. Taking out his journal, Joseph drew a map of the creek. He marked the place where his brothers were buried. Someday he would come back and put a marker on their grave. He didn't think it was wise to do so now. He also marked the place where the money was buried.

He would create a new life for himself and wait to see if anyone searched for him. He would change his name so that he would be harder to find. He would find a job keeping books for a business in a new town. He needed to change everything he could about his life. He would come back for the money when he was sure he was safe.

Joseph saddled his horse and loaded the other horses with what was left of the supplies. He would ride west until he found a town. There he would sell the extra saddles and horses and buy supplies. Then he would travel further west until he found a little town where he could find a job and settle down. With that goal in mind, he rode away from all he had ever known and Paradise Creek.

SHERIFF BLAKE WAS in his office silently berating himself for losing Joseph's trail. *That boy wasn't so green after all. He and his brothers are probably halfway to Mexico by now*, he thought.

"Sheriff! Sheriff!"

"Mornin' Otis. What can I do for you?"

"The posse just came back to town."

"Guess I'd better go see what they found then."

The weary posse rode into Willow and stopped at the saloon. They were describing the events to the locals who were listening in hopes of their money being returned.

"I tell you that money has to be somewhere along Paradise Creek," said Adams. "It can't be anywhere else."

"Tell me what happened, Clay."

"Sheriff, we found those Keys boys sleeping under a big tree near Paradise Creek, but we didn't find the money. We searched until a thunderstorm blew up. We decided then to ride into Vernon for the night."

"Where are the Keys brothers now?"

For the first time, Clay seemed to feel a little guilty about what they had done. He hung his head and said nothing.

"I see. Does the sheriff in Vernon know what happened?"

"No. Well, maybe. He may have been in the saloon when we were in there talking about it"

"All right, I'll get word to him just to make sure. Did you bury them?"

"No, we didn't have time. We left them both hanging in that big tree?"

"Both? There were only two there?"

"Yep, Frank and Harold. Who else would have been there?"

"Their brother Joseph rode out of town right after you boys did. I lost his trail just before dark."

"You didn't find the money?"

"No, Otis. We didn't find any of it," one of the posse members replied.

"Sheriff, what are you going to do? I demand that you find that money!"

"Otis, the Keys twins are dead. If they took the money, they took the location of it with them to their graves."

"That boy! He must have it! Find him Sheriff!"

"Were there two thieves or three Otis? You said there were only two. We watched that boy from the time you reported the theft until I lost his trail in the hills. It isn't likely he could have met with his brothers during that time."

Otis Turner dared not say more. The sheriff might suspect that he knew the truth. He would go to jail if he told the sheriff what really happened.

He would be ruined if the money was not recovered. His reputation had already begun to suffer. There had been no new deposits made since the robbery. He could go to Paradise Creek, but he had no idea where to begin his search particularly since he didn't know who had taken the money from under his desk.

Having lost the trust of the citizens of Willow, the bank closed. Disgraced and ashamed, Otis Turner gathered his belongings and left Willow under the cover of darkness.

Sheriff Blake sent word to the Wilbarger County sheriff informing him of the lynching and where it took place. He also informed him of the missing money presumed to be buried somewhere near the creek. A few weeks later he received a reply.

Sheriff Blake,

I went to the location near Paradise Creek. I found the big tree with cut ropes hanging from it but no bodies. After a search of the area, I found a large patch of freshly dug earth that turned out to be a grave site for two men. I found no evidence of the missing money.

Sincerely,

Sheriff Gates

Sheriff Blake wondered about Joseph. *Did he have the money all along and let his brothers die for him? That doesn't seem likely. Maybe Joseph joined them, but if so, the posse should have found him. He probably found his brothers after they were hung. He must have buried them. Where is he now? Does he have the money?*

Clay Adams made plans to return to Paradise Creek and continue searching for the money. He sold his ranch, bought the land where the Keys brothers died, and moved his family there. Every spare moment he had was spent searching for the lost money. One morning while digging on the creek bank, he took his last breath when his heart stopped beating.

As time went by, the story of the hidden money grew. The

amount grew larger and became gold instead of currency. The story of the robbery circulated for years and became local legend. Treasure hunters searched Paradise creek and the surrounding area but found nothing. Gradually, the fortune hunters stopped coming and Paradise Creek was peaceful again.

FOUR

Lizzie Fletcher was busy packing. She was finally taking a vacation. She was going home for the first time since she had moved to Chicago five years earlier. It was hard to believe it was already June 2010. She had planned to go back to visit many times, but her job as assistant events coordinator at one of Chicago's prominent hotels didn't leave her much free time. The little free time she did have was spent with Rob Banyon. Lizzie met Rob when he stayed at the hotel to arrange a business convention.

"You know the term Greek god comes to mind every time I see that man," Celia said.

"Celia, I can't think about him like that and work with him. How would I concentrate?"

"I'm glad you're working with him so that I can just look at him." Celia grinned as she reached for the ringing phone on the desk.

"Celia, you should wipe the drool from your chin before a guest sees you."

Celia flipped her off and answered the phone.

Celia was short and plump with an infectious laugh, dancing blue eyes, and a winning smile. She chose to express herself with color, lots of it from head to toe. Since she wore a hotel uniform while at work, her love of color was expressed in her hair, nails, and the occasional print scarf.

Rob was tall and tan with an athletic build. His hair was blonde and tended to fall down over his left eye. His eyes were hazel with a twinkle of friendliness. When he entered a room, his smile seemed to light every corner.

The friendship between Lizzie and Rob grew as they spent time together planning the convention. After the convention was over, Rob asked Lizzie out to dinner. He had an office and apartment in both Chicago and New York. His time was split between the two cities. Over the past year, they had gone out whenever he was in Chicago.

One evening while at dinner, Rob told her that he had been married. Tears welled up in his eyes as he showed her a photograph of his wife and two girls. He told Lizzie that they had been killed two years earlier in a car accident. His wife was a beautiful brunette with a gorgeous smile and kind brown eyes. Both his daughters looked like their mother. They had been twelve and eight when the accident happened. He was obviously devoted to his family and still felt their loss deeply. Lizzie thought that was probably the moment she began to fall in love with him.

It had been only a month since they had spent a wonderful weekend together. They were lying in bed enjoying the morning when Rob slipped a ring on her finger and asked her to marry him. After a few speechless moments, she said yes. They had decided that August would be the best month to be married. The actual date was still up in the air.

Rob didn't really want Lizzie to leave. He had spent the night at her apartment so that he could see her before she left.

"I'll miss you so much," he had told her. "The wedding isn't until the 26th. Why do you have to be there an entire week? I'll be in New York when you get home next week."

"Jan asked me to be her maid of honor. She's my cousin; we grew up together. I can't let her down. Besides, I haven't been home since I moved here. I need to spend some time with my family."

"I know. I understand, but I don't have to like it." He smiled that smile that always melted her heart.

"I'll miss you, too. I wish you could go with me. I haven't told my family about you yet. It would be a big surprise for you to walk in with me."

"I would be glad to go if I didn't have to be here for an important meeting," he paused. "You could wait to tell them about me until I can go too couldn't you? I'd like to ask your dad for permission to marry you."

Lizzie hugged and kissed him. "Daddy will love that. I won't spoil it, but I don't like keeping the fact that I'm engaged and moving to New York from them. You'll have to meet them soon."

"Have you told the hotel that you're quitting?"

"Not yet, but I will when I get back from Texas and I'll inform the apartment manager that I won't be renewing my lease. I'll have a lot of packing to do."

"I have vacation time coming soon. We'll arrange to meet your family, then, I promise," Rob assured her. He looked at his watch. "OH SHIT! Is that the time? I'm going to be late if I don't leave now. Don't forget to look over those papers while you're gone and think about setting a wedding date. I'll see you later; call me!" With that, Rob rushed out the door.

Lizzie finished packing and took a cab to the airport. She would fly to Dallas and then rent a car for the remainder of the trip to Vernon. Its population was under twelve thousand people, but there were many people outside the city limits on farms and ranches. Her family owned a farm southwest of town.

After claiming her bags, Lizzie took a shuttle to Avis and rented a car. She dialed Rob's cell phone while she waited. When he didn't answer, she left a message on his voicemail telling him she had arrived safely in Dallas and would call him again later. She was going to be away for only a week, but she already missed Rob terribly.

She didn't mind the drive because it gave her some time alone. She didn't expect to have any alone time once she reached her parents' house. She almost ached at the thought of seeing them again. She promised herself she would come home more often. She thought about home and Rob. She was sure her family would like him.

With an hour left in her journey, Lizzie's cell phone rang. She was a little disappointed to see that it was Jan instead of Rob. Stopping at a roadside park, Lizzie returned the call.

"Hi, Jan. This is Lizzie."

"Lizzie, you sound so good! I can't wait to see you! Where are you?"

Jan always talked in rush when she was excited. She didn't give a person a chance to answer before she moved on to the next question. Lizzie replied when Jan stopped to catch her breath.

"I just drove through Wichita Falls. What's up?"

"I know you probably want to go to your house, but would you mind stopping in town first? We need to see if your dress is going to fit. We can go to the dress shop together, or I can meet you there."

"I'll meet you there in about an hour."

"Sounds great, see you then, and thanks Lizzie."

Lizzie laughed. "I'll see you there."

Lizzie arrived at the dress shop to see Jan waiting for her outside. Noticing her engagement ring was still on her finger, she slipped it off and into her purse before opening the car door. She climbed out of the car right into a bear hug from Jan. After many tearful hugs, how are you, and so glad to see you, they went inside.

The dress needed only a few alterations. Bridesmaid's dresses are commonly thought to be unattractive, but Jan had excellent taste. She chose a style that would flatter all of her attendants. Lizzie hardly recognized herself. She was petite with straight shoulder length red hair, vivid blue eyes, and a few freckles across her pert little nose. She always felt that she was awkward and a little boyish. But now, she saw a grown sophisticated woman in the mirror.

Jan sighed. "You look beautiful."

After a moment she said, "If you don't mind, I'd like for you to see my dress while we're here."

"I don't mind a bit. I'd love to get a preview."

Both women went into the dressing rooms to change. Lizzie finished changing and waited for Jan.

Jan came carefully out of the dressing room and stood on a small platform.

"Jan, you are absolutely gorgeous. Eli will faint when he sees you walking down the aisle."

Jan beamed with pleasure. "I don't think it needs any more alterations do you?"

"It fits like a glove. I wouldn't change a thing."

After the fittings were completed, the two women left the shop and walked toward their cars.

"Lizzie, how about we go for an ice cream cone like we used to."

"Oh, that sounds so good," Lizzie sighed. She thought for a moment about fitting into the bridesmaid dress and then said, "Why not? Get in!" They drove to their favorite ice cream shop and ordered.

Jan Pearson was brunette, slightly taller than her cousin with the same vivid blue eyes. She was two months older than Lizzie. They had grown up and gone to school together. Jan's mother and Lizzie's mother were sisters.

The two cousins laughed and enjoyed their ice cream talking about things they did when they were young. They talked about the wedding and Lizzie couldn't help noticing the worried expression that had crept across Jan's face.

"Okay, what's wrong? You look like you have something on your mind."

"Lizzie, I'm sorry I didn't tell you before, but I didn't know myself until yesterday. I didn't call you because I was afraid you wouldn't come."

"Jan, nothing was going to keep me from coming to your wedding. What could be so terrible?"

Jan hesitated a moment and then in a rush said, "Drake is coming. He's going to be Eli's best man. If you would rather not stand opposite Drake or walk out with him, I completely understand. You can be a bridesmaid, and I'll ask Faith to be my maid of honor."

Jan stopped for a breath and watched Lizzie with a mixture of hope and dread. Hope that Lizzie would at least stay for the wedding and dread that she would go back to Chicago on the next flight.

Lizzie sat in stunned silence for a moment. She had pushed all thoughts of Drake Wagner from her mind. Of course, he would come to his brother's wedding. When she saw the look on Jan's face, she was tempted to tell her about Rob to ease her mind.

"It's okay Jan. I'll still be your maid of honor. As long as Drake and Megan are okay with the idea, then, I am too."

Jan breathed a sigh of relief and again in a rush said, "I'm so sorry. When Eli said one of his brothers was going to be his best man, I assumed it would be Gage. Drake left town a few months after you did and hasn't been back."

"I thought he and Megan were going to settle here and work on the family farm."

It was Jan's turn to be stunned. "Oh! You mean you don't know?"

"Know what?" Lizzie asked.

"It's a really long story, and I don't know all of the details. Drake didn't marry Megan."

After saying goodnight to Jan, Lizzie drove out to the family farm. Just the sight of it made her heart ache. This was her Tara, the place where she found peace and healing. It was her home, and it always would be no matter how far she roamed.

She stopped in the drive. Before she could get her door open, her parents and her grandmother were hurrying toward her. Hugs and tears were shared while everyone talked at the same time. Eventually, Lizzie and her dad took her things upstairs to her old room. She hugged him again.

"I've missed you, Daddy. I'm sorry I've haven't been home."

"I've missed you too, honey."

They hugged again, and Lizzie said, "I'll be down in a minute. I need to freshen up a bit."

James Fletcher smiled as he closed her door and went downstairs.

Lizzie bounded down the stairs as she had when she was younger. She had changed into shorts and her favorite t-shirt. She stood in the doorway looking at her family for a moment before running over to the table and giving them each another hug.

"I've missed you all so much. I promise I won't stay away so long again."

"You'd better not young lady. Your old granny might not be here if stay away another five years."

"Granny, you're going to be here for another fifty years at least."

Lois Fletcher beamed at her granddaughter. "I'm glad your home, sweetie."

"I am too, Granny."

"Mama, what's wrong?"

Ellen Fletcher was wiping tears from her eyes with the back of her hand. "Can't I cry when my baby girl comes home for a visit?"

"I'd prefer you didn't," Lizzie said giving her a peck on the cheek.

Ellen smiled and took a cherry cobbler out of the oven. It was Lizzie's favorite. They sat at the kitchen table talking, eating cobbler, and drinking coffee as they had when Lizzie was in college. It was almost as though she had never left.

Lizzie was the only child of James and Ellen Fletcher. She had inherited her red hair from her dad and her blue eyes from her mother. She inherited her spirit from her grandmother.

Ellen worked in town as a librarian and planned to retire at the end of the year. James worked the family farm. Granny, James' mother, lived a short distance from James and Ellen in the large house where she grew up. She had been retired for many years, but she helped on the farm, driving vehicles and equipment from place to place.

Lizzie told her family about her job and her coworkers. She told them about her apartment and showed them photos of different parts of Chicago. They told her about all the people she knew that were still there and those that had moved away. They told her about almost everyone. Everyone except Drake. She could feel a little bit of tension when they discussed the wedding.

"I met Jan in town to have my dress fitted. She told me that Drake would be there. I know that I never wanted to talk about him, but it will be okay. I've moved on. That's all in the past."

There was a moment of silence and then audible sighs of relief. "We're so glad, sweetie. That was such a painful time for you," Ellen said.

"It was, but it's over, and I survived. The truth is that I wouldn't be where I am now if Drake and I had gotten married."

"That's true dear. Have you seen him or heard from him since then?"

"No Granny, I haven't. I didn't know that he hadn't married Megan until Jan told me."

"Well, that was sad, but I think that turned out for the best. Drake moved away to follow his dream. Megan had moved away too. I heard that she married a local boy and has moved back into this area."

"It doesn't matter now, Granny. That part of my life is finished."

"What do you think it will be like when you see him again for the first time?"

Lizzie thought about it for a moment before answering. "I don't know, Mama. I hadn't thought about that. It would be nice if we could be friends. I guess I'll have to wait and see."

"I know what I'd like to say to him when I see him again."

"James, you can't do that. It's all over and done with."

"I know Ellen, but I'd still like to kick his ass."

"Daddy, I'm over it, and I'm fine. You don't need to kick his ass." Lizzie laughed.

James grumbled a little and looked embarrassed as he grinned at his daughter. "You shouldn't use language like that." The room erupted in laughter.

"Is there a young man there in Chicago that has helped you to move on?" Granny winked as she asked.

Lizzie blushed. "I wasn't going to say anything until he could come with me to meet y'all. Please don't tell anyone else and act surprised when you meet him. His name is Rob and we've been seeing each other for almost a year." She left out the part about being engaged so that she didn't completely break her promise.

After sharing all the details about Rob that she felt comfortable sharing with her family, they all said goodnight and retired for the evening. Lizzie thought that they felt better after they found out about him. Lizzie called her fiancé before climbing into bed.

"Hello sweetheart."

"Hi, how was your day?"

"Long and dull. I've been home only a few minutes and was about to call you. I'm glad you made it safely. Where are you now?"

"I'm at mom and dad's house. I'm about to go to bed."

"How was your trip?"

Lizzie told him about the flight and all that she had done since landing in Dallas.

"I'll be in meetings all day tomorrow," he said. "I'll call you when I get home."

"Okay, I'll talk to you then."

"I love you, baby."

"I love you too, goodnight."

Lizzie smiled to herself as she thought about Rob. She was thinking about him and the life they would have together when her mother's question ran through her mind. *What do you think it will be like when you see him again for the first time?*

She had never thought about it since she never expected to see him again. She had pushed Drake Wagner and the time they had together out of her mind. It seemed impossible to push all that away now that she was here. Here in the place where it happened.

FIVE

After graduating from Vernon High School in 2001, Lizzie moved to Wichita Falls to study at Midwestern State University. She lived in the dorms the first year and worked waiting tables while going to school. She majored in hotel and restaurant management and dreamed of one day owning her own inn.

Faith Wagner was a tall, willowy brunette with green eyes, high cheek bones and a perfect complexion. She had been told more than once that she could have been a model. That kind of life didn't appeal to her. She was a country girl at heart and worked on the family farm alongside her four brothers. Faith was studying business management and wanted someday to own her own company. She lived next door to Lizzie in the dorm, and they became close friends. Faith would occasionally go home with Lizzie for a visit and in turn Lizzie would visit Faith's home.

Megan Ford was the youngest of three daughters born to Roxanne and the late Collin Ford. She was a blue eyed blonde with an hourglass figure that turned every man's head. She lived down the hall from Lizzie and Faith. Megan was working toward a degree in general studies. She wasn't really sure what she wanted to be other than rich. Her dream was to become rich and famous with as little effort as possible. She also wanted to marry a rich man. She followed Lizzie and Faith around in an effort to meet one of Faith's brothers. She mistakenly believed that Faith's family owned the Waggoner ranch south of Vernon.

Ben and Carol Wagner owned and operated a small farm near Chillicothe, a town north of Vernon. They had five children: Drake, Eli, Faith, Gage, and Hart. They weren't wealthy, but they were comfortable. It was on one of the weekend visits to Faith's home that Lizzie met Drake. They had an instant connection and began dating right away.

Drake was six feet tall with the same dark hair and green eyes that his sister had. He was strong and muscular from farm work. He was almost finished with his college studies in forestry and agricultural business. He dreamed that one day he would be able to live in the mountains and work with the forestry service.

Drake had stayed to help with the family farm after he received his bachelor's degree. His family was pretty sure that he stayed because he was in love with Lizzie. The couple had been dating for four years, and Drake had secretly been saving money to buy an engagement ring. They had been talking about getting married for months, and Lizzie would be graduating soon.

In March of 2005, Drake was the best man and organizer of the bachelor party for his closest friend, Cole Lindsay. Drake, the groom, and several others that attended were too drunk to remember what happened for the majority of the party.

Drake recalled waking up on one side of a corner booth to find Cole passed out on the other side. He had dragged Cole out to the truck and drove him home to try and sober up in time for his wedding.

It was only a week before Lizzie, Faith, and the rest of the class of 2005 were to receive their degrees. Drake hesitated before knocking on the door of Lizzie and Faith's apartment. He felt nauseous and wondered how he was going to break the news. Lizzie answered the door.

"We need to talk," he said.

"What's wrong?" Lizzie asked before she let him in the door. Drake looked so worried that it concerned her.

"Is Faith here?"

"No, she won't be back for a while. What's wrong?"

"Maybe we should sit down," Drake suggested. They sat down on the little sofa in the living room.

"Please, listen until I've finished. I don't think I'll get through it if you don't."

"Okay," Lizzie replied. She was scared now.

"There's no easy way to tell you this, so I'll just say it." He paused and took a deep breath. "Megan Ford came to see me this afternoon. She says she's pregnant," he hesitated, "with my child."

Lizzie's heart stopped. She felt the room spinning. When her heart started again, it hammered in her chest. "WHAT? That isn't possible. Why would she say that?"

"Let me finish, please Lizzie." He took another deep breath and then said in a rush, "She was waitressing at the bar where we had Cole's bachelor party. She said we slept together during the party. I was so drunk, Lizzie; I don't even remember talking to her." Drake watched Lizzie's face hoping she would understand.

"It's not possible! She's lying! She has to be!" She could practically hear her heart breaking. The thought of Drake sleeping with another woman was too painful to be true.

"I know she's probably lying, but what if she isn't. What if she is really carrying my child?"

Lizzie was shaking. She got up and walked around the room with her hands on her head. *This is all a dream; a very bad dream. It can't be happening. Drake told me he loves me. I love him. We've been together for years and never cheated on each other. We've been making plans for a future together. It can't be true. Megan can't be carrying Drake's child.*

"Please, Lizzie, sit down."

She could hear the anguish in his voice. She sat down and listened, speechless as Drake continued.

"I've been checking into paternity testing. The party was in March, so she can't be more than two months pregnant. It will be at least another two months before a paternity test can be done. If she refuses to have it done, we'll have to wait until the baby is born."

"Drake, I have to know," tears were streaming down Lizzie's face. She could hardly breathe when she asked, "Did you sleep with her?"

Drake looked at Lizzie his own pain showing in his face, tears in his eyes. "Lizzie, I love you, and I want to tell you there is no way in hell that I slept with Megan. I just don't remember."

"I see," Lizzie sobbed. "What if you are the father?"

"I've been driving around for hours trying to figure this out. I don't see any other way. I've got to do the right thing."

"Are we supposed to put our lives on hold until we find out if the baby is yours?"

"Will you do that Lizzie? Will you wait for me?"

Lizzie searched for the right words before she spoke. She knew Drake was an honorable man and doing what he believed to be right was a part of who he was.

"What are you saying?"

"I'm saying that we can't get married until I find out for sure if I'm the father. I'm so sorry, Lizzie. This is tearing me apart. I don't want to let you go, but I have to do what's right. If that is my child, I have to take responsibility."

They held each other tight and cried for a long time. Finally, he kissed her. "I love you Lizzie."

Lizzie sobbed, "I love you too."

Somehow Lizzie managed to get through the next few days and graduation. She barely remembered any of it now. She went through the motions during the days afterward. She and Drake saw each other often, but plans for the future were never mentioned. Their time together was filled with doubt and worry.

One evening after dinner, Drake told her that Megan had refused to have a paternity test.

"What are we going to do?"

"Lizzie, I've been thinking about it. Megan might agree to a paternity test if I ask her to marry me."

Lizzie was screaming inside but struggled to remain outwardly calm. "What if she says yes and still refuses the test?"

"It will be a long engagement, and the test will be done after the baby is born."

"What if the baby is yours Drake? What then?" Lizzie was unable to contain herself any longer and began to cry with pain and anger.

Drake sadly lowered his head. He was torn between what he wanted and what he believed to be right. "I have to do the right thing, Lizzie. I don't want my child to grow up without a father."

"Am I supposed to wait around until the baby is born while you're engaged to marry someone else? What am I supposed to do if you find out that you slept with her after all? I love you Drake, but I can't stay here and watch you with someone else."

Drake glared at her. "You believe I slept with her? You believe I would cheat on you? You know I love you Lizzie!"

"Can you tell me without a doubt that you didn't sleep with her? Can you tell me positively that Megan's baby isn't yours?" Lizzie shouted.

"You know I can't!" Drake shouted back.

Lizzie took a few deep breaths to calm down before she said, "I have a job interview in Chicago next week. If I'm offered the job, I'm going to take it."

Drake was astonished. "You're just going to leave me? With no thought to our plans or how much I love you?"

"You're going to propose to Megan? With no thought to our plans or how much I love you?" Lizzie replied angrily.

Drake sighed. His heart ached. He was silent for a moment and then dejectedly he said, "Point taken."

Drake took Lizzie in his arms. They held each other close, crying. Finally, Lizzie stepped back.

"Goodbye, Drake," she said wiping tears from her face.

"Goodbye, Lizzie. I'll always love you." He kissed her on the cheek and walked out the door wiping his own tears.

She told her family that it was too painful. She didn't want to talk about Drake or hear his name again. She began pushing him and the entire incident out of her mind.

Slowly, she started picking up the pieces of her life. When she was offered the job in Chicago, she packed up and moved the following day. She needed to get away from Vernon and the painful memories. She told herself she'd come back for visits with her family, but she hadn't.

Jan had told Lizzie the rest of the story while they were having ice cream. She sat in silent amazement as the truth unfolded.

Megan had been waitressing at the bar the night of the bachelor party. She made a move on Drake, but he rejected her. She was angry and began drinking heavily. She slept with another man at the party and discovered a month later that she was pregnant. She had no idea who the father was. When she heard that Drake couldn't remember anything about that night, she decided to name him as the father. She was expecting lots of money for child support; after all a wealthy man like Drake Wagner could afford it.

Drake proposed to Megan the day after Lizzie left for Chicago. Megan was surprised and pleased at the proposal. This could mean a lot more than just child support. She accepted but thought he could have afforded a much bigger diamond.

Drake delayed setting a date for the wedding as he had planned. He began investigating what had happened at the bachelor party. He talked with people who were working at the bar and with some of the other men that were there that night. Some of the things Megan had told him just didn't add up.

Megan was six months pregnant when she began having strong contractions one morning. She dismissed them as false labor. Her friends had arranged an engagement party for that evening, and she didn't want anything to spoil it. She was looking forward to flaunting her new found wealth in front of her family and friends.

Drake had had a prenuptial agreement drawn up and took it to Megan the afternoon of the engagement party. She glanced at it and said, "Why do we need this?"

"We need a prenup as a precaution to protect our respective family assets. My parents asked us all to have one before we marry," he lied. "Read it and make note of anything that needs to be corrected. We'll have the final draft ready to sign the week before the wedding."

"We haven't even set a date yet," Megan said as she rubbed her growing belly. "We can't put it off much longer."

"Just read it, please. I need to get back to work. I'll see you at the party."

Megan had another contraction. She tossed the agreement aside when it passed and began to dress for the party.

That night at the engagement party, the contractions began again. They were so intense that Megan collapsed. Roxanne and Drake rushed her to the hospital. The doctor decided to keep her for observation.

Megan was deep in thought when she began to feel better. Her wealthy soon to be in-laws could have dressed nicer for her party. *I suppose they might have been trying to keep a low profile*, she told herself.

Drake walked into the room. "How are you feeling?"

"Better, darling. I hate being in this hospital. Take me home."

"Dr. Hughes wants to keep you under observation overnight."

"I don't want to stay here until tomorrow."

"Well, you don't have a choice. Did you read the prenup?"

"No, I was too excited about the party. We don't need a silly old prenup anyway."

"I've already explained why we need one. Read it and make corrections," he said handing her another copy of the agreement. "I won't set a wedding date until this is signed."

"Oh, all right. Let me see it." Megan read for a few minutes and then said, "I see a mistake already."

"Where?" Drake asked.

"Your last name is misspelled. Whoever typed this must be a total idiot."

Drake looked at the document.

"No, Megan. My name is W-A-G-N-E-R."

"What?" Megan's jaw dropped in astonishment. All this time she thought Drake and his family were wealthy. "Why didn't you tell me?"

"You've known my sister for years. I thought you knew." Drake smiled to himself as he turned and left the room. "I'll see you in the morning," he called over his shoulder. Megan cringed with another strong contraction.

The contractions continued for several hours. Drake was called back to the hospital late that night. The little boy was stillborn in the early hours of the following morning. Drake pulled the doctor aside and privately asked for a paternity test.

Megan mourned the loss of her plans more than the loss of her child. *Drake isn't rich. How could I have been so stupid? Will he still marry me now that there's no baby? He has too. I'm pretty sure that I might be in love with him.*

Drake went to see Megan only once after she left the hospital. He wasn't going to marry her, but he wanted to wait for the test results before telling her. Megan had called him several times. He told her he was working and that he would see her when he was free. A message was waiting for him when he checked his voicemail a week later. The results of the paternity test were in Dr. Hughes' office.

Drake drove into town. Dr. Hughes met him at the door and handed him the report. "I don't know what you were hoping to hear, but you weren't the father of Megan's baby."

"That's what I thought. May I have a copy of this?"

"I've made several for you just in case you should need them."

Drake took the copies, thanked the doctor, and got into his truck. He phoned Faith, told her about the test results, and asked her to meet him at the shopping center. He needed someone with him so that he wouldn't lose control when he confronted Megan. He was angry, angrier than he could remember being in his entire life. Megan had destroyed all of his hopes, his dreams, and most importantly his relationship with Lizzie.

He waited for Faith in the shopping center parking lot and thought about Lizzie. He wanted to see her and tell her everything that had happened. He wanted to beg her forgiveness, but he knew that he had hurt her so deeply that she would never forgive him. He could ask her family how to get in touch with her, but he dismissed the thought. They had also been hurt by Megan's lies. They had begun to call him their future son-in-law and treated him like a son. He couldn't face them.

When Faith arrived, they drove to Megan's house. He was sure she wouldn't object to ending their engagement since she knew he was not who she thought. He had a copy of the paternity test with him just in case.

Megan surprised him. She insisted that he marry her. "I'll sue for breach of promise and take you for everything you've got. Oh and there won't be any prenup!"

"You're right, Megan. There will be no prenup and no law suit. The wedding is off." Drake said shaking with anger as he handed Megan the copy of the paternity test results. "You lied to me. You ruined my life." He wanted to say a lot more, but Faith, seeing the look on his face, put her hand on his arm and gently said, "Drake, she isn't worth it."

He took Megan's left hand. She tried to pull away, but he held it firmly. He took the engagement ring off her finger, turned on his heel, and walked out the door. Megan started screaming as the door swung shut. He grinned at Faith and said, "Let's go home Sis."

Drake began applying for jobs in areas where he could put his degree to work. A month after the breakup with Megan, he left for Colorado to work in the forestry service.

SIX

Lizzie woke Saturday morning to the smell of coffee brewing. She hadn't realized how much she missed waking up to that smell. She always had coffee after she got to work. She went downstairs to find Ellen and Lois sitting at the kitchen table.

"Good morning, Mama. Good morning, Granny," she said as she planted a kiss on each woman's cheek. "Where's Daddy?"

"He had to get started moving the cattle to the east pasture. He said he'd be missing a lot of work since we'll be in town for Jan's festivities later this week," Ellen explained.

"Lizzie, sit down; I want to talk to you about something," Lois said.

"Okay. It sounds like something serious Granny."

"Well, it is in a way. Is your job in Chicago the kind of job you always dreamed about?"

"No, it isn't. It's a work my way up the ladder and pay my dues kind of job."

"Would you still like to run your own inn?"

"That has always been my dream, but I don't see it happening anytime soon."

"All right then. I have a proposition for you. I'm getting too old to live in that great big house all alone. You're parents and I have been talking about this, and we want to see what you think. We'll turn the house over to you. You can renovate it and make it into the inn you've always dreamed of owning."

"But, Granny..."

"Now, let me finish," Granny interrupted." I'll move in here with James and Ellen. You'll manage the inn. I'll fund the renovations, within reason mind you. Your parents and I will help when you need it. The old place needs fixing up anyway, and I see no reason to fix it up only for one old lady. It will become a family business." Granny paused for a moment, and then said, "Well what do you think?"

Lizzie didn't know what to say. She wanted to jump at the chance to design and run her own inn. But she was to be married and planned to move to New York. She didn't want to say no, but she couldn't say yes.

"Wow! I didn't see that coming at all." She paused and then said, "That is such a great idea, but I really need to think about it for a while. Granny, are you sure you want to give up your home?"

"Lizzie, your daddy and I think it's best for your grandmother to move in here with us. The old house needs a lot of repair. It worries us to have your granny there all alone with the house in that condition."

"I can't take care of the place anymore, and I hate to see it go to ruin. Promise me you'll think about it."

"I will Granny. I promise. I'd like to go and look around over there. I haven't been to your house in so long."

"We'll have a look around when we get back from town. The bride's luncheon starts in a couple of hours. We'd better hurry if we're going to make it on time," Granny said.

At the luncheon, Lizzie saw Faith Wagner for the first time since she had moved away. They had been good friends but hadn't spoken since the breakup with Drake.

They hugged and talked a few minutes when Faith asked, "Are you okay with seeing Drake?"

"I'm okay with it if he is. That was a long time ago."

Faith smiled, "He said practically the same thing."

Others at the luncheon were girls she had known in school but not well. They seemed to be whispering about her when she looked in their direction. She suspected it was about the upcoming face to face with Drake. She chose to ignore them and enjoy the day.

Lizzie stood up tapping her glass with her spoon. "May I have your attention ladies? There is a rumor that the men have planned a bachelor party for the groom. I've been out of touch with things around here. It's sort of a last minute situation, but it seems to me that a bachelorette party is in order."

Everyone cheered and applauded their approval. Lizzie continued, "As maid of honor, I know that it's my responsibility, but I'm going to need some help to put this together in such a short time."

"Lizzie you really don't have to do that. I don't need a bachelorette party."

"Of course you do, doesn't she ladies!" Lizzie waited for the cheers and applause to subside. "Besides we can't let the boys have all the fun."

Plans for the bachelorette party were made for Thursday evening so that everyone could look their best for the wedding on Saturday. Lizzie's calendar for the week was soon filling up. Final dress fittings were to be on Tuesday afternoon. A family dinner was planned for Wednesday evening. The rehearsal and rehearsal dinner were to be Friday evening. The wedding was on Saturday. She was scheduled to return to Chicago on Sunday and back at work Monday morning.

"Lizzie?"

"I'm in the kitchen, Granny."

"Are you ready to take a look at my house?"

"Let me get something to make notes with, and I'll be ready to go."

Lizzie went upstairs. She rummaged through her old desk and found a notepad and pencil. She went back down the stairs and out to her car where her grandmother waited.

They drove the half mile to Granny's home. Lois Cline Fletcher was born in the old house. She and her husband, Stewart, had bought her siblings' share of the property so that now she had sole ownership. She and Stewart had worked the land and raised their children, James and Grace, there. James worked the land now.

"I don't want to disturb you, so I'll just wait here in the living room. Poke around all you want."

"I won't be long, Granny."

Lizzie walked through every room of the house and around the outside. She made note of needed repairs and changes that would have to be made if it were to become an inn. Her great, great grandfather had bought the land and built the house when her great grandfather was very young. Rooms had been added to accommodate the children born to her great grandparents. Trees had been planted around the farm by each generation. Some of those trees had grown to shade the house in hot summer days, and others had proven to be protection from the winds that seemed to blow constantly.

Lizzie returned to the living room where her grandmother waited.

"What do you think?"

"Lots of changes will need to be made, but it has potential. I have some ideas, but I'll need time to make sketches and work things out."

"Do you think you could make it work?"

"I'll have to think about it, Granny. It would be a big step."

"Think about it as long as you need to. We should be getting back." Granny winked at her and said, "I'll bet your mama has another cherry cobbler about to come out of the oven."

The rest of Lizzie's week was too busy to make sketches or plans for the old house. She visited with old friends and relatives between appointments. The final fittings for the bride's maids were completed, and the bachelorette party had been a success.

Lizzie dressed for the wedding rehearsal and checked her reflection in the mirror. She thought about calling Rob again but changed her mind. She had talked with him yesterday. He said he would call her when he arrived in New York.

She was nervous about facing Drake. She was in love with Rob now, but she was worried. How would she feel when she saw him? How would he feel? What would they say to each other? She tried to push those thoughts and her nervousness aside. She would be fine. She would think of him as an old friend she hadn't seen in years.

Jan and Lizzie arrived at the church at the same moment. "Are you ready?" Jan asked.

"I'm ready."

"Let's go in. It'll be much cooler inside," Jan said as she took Lizzie's arm and led her into the sanctuary.

They were the first to arrive and were admiring the decor for the wedding. An arch stood above the altar lined with twinkle lights, silver ribbon, yellow silk roses, and white silk daisies. Twinkle lights lined the walls. The pews had small silk bouquets of roses and daises attached with ribbon to each end.

"Ahem," someone cleared his throat. The women turned to see Eli and his brothers, Gage and Hart, standing at the entrance to the sanctuary. Jan went to Eli and gave him a quick kiss.

"Where's Drake," she whispered.

Eli whispered back, "He's talking with Reverend Stevenson outside. Are you sure she's okay?"

"I think so. Is he?"

"Looks like we're about to find out."

Lizzie was talking with Gage and Hart when Drake came in with the Reverend.

Drake saw Lizzie before she saw him. *She's more beautiful than I remembered. I wonder if she's as nervous as I am.*

Lizzie's heart skipped a beat when she saw him. *He looks good. He probably isn't nervous at all.*

After an awkward pause as they looked at each other, Drake was the first to speak.

"Hello, Lizzie. How are you?"

"Hi, Drake. I'm good. How are you?"

"Good. Are you in town long?"

"I'm leaving Sunday. I have to be back at work Monday morning."

"Oh well, I bet your folks wish you could stay longer."

"They probably do. How long are you going to be able to stay?"

"I'm here for two weeks."

"That's good. You'll have time to relax and catch up with everyone."

"I think it's about time we start the rehearsal everyone," Reverend Stevenson interrupted.

After rehearsing several times, the group left the church and met again for the rehearsal dinner at one of the local restaurants. Lizzie was thankful that she wasn't seated next to Drake. Their first meeting had gone smoothly, but she couldn't think of anything else to say to him. She wasn't sure what her feelings were about him at the moment and needed to sort them out.

She lay awake that night thinking about Drake. She felt that she had seen an old friend for the first time in years, but there was something else. Walking down the aisle together at rehearsal had made her feel something that she couldn't describe. She had put the pain behind her, but she was still attracted to him. She finally came to the conclusion that she would always be attracted to him, but it didn't mean that she still loved him.

She thought of Rob and their plans for the future. *Why hasn't he called? He should have arrived in New York by now.* She dialed his cell phone number and got his voicemail. She sighed and tried to sleep. Tomorrow would be a busy day.

The wedding was perfect. Jan was stunningly beautiful. Eli was terribly handsome. They were so happy that Lizzie suspected their faces would be sore the next day from all the smiles.

At the reception, Lizzie danced most of the evening. She danced once with Eli and several dances with Gage and Hart. She danced with her dad and Jan's dad. She was about to sit down when Drake asked her to dance. They danced a few dances, but neither asked the other what they really wanted to know.

As another song started, Lizzie said, "Oh can we sit this one out? My feet are killing me."

"Okay, we can catch up a little. We haven't had a chance to talk," Drake replied.

"No we haven't." Lizzie said apprehensively. She wasn't sure why that made her nervous.

They sat at a nearby table and struggled for something to say. "Are you still in Chicago?" Drake finally asked. Lizzie told him that she was and told him about her job and the city.

"Where do you live?"

"I'm living in Denver," he said. He told her about his work and how much he liked living there.

"Are you married?"

"No, but I have been seeing someone for a while now," Lizzie answered. "Are you?"

"No, I was seeing a nice woman but it didn't work out."

"I'm sorry to hear that."

"Are you happy, Lizzie?"

Lizzie smiled. "I am. Are you?"

Drake smiled back at her and said, "Yes. I'm sorry about the way things happened between us. I would take it all back if I could."

"I know. I'm sorry too. Jan told me about Megan."

"I'm glad that turned out the way it did." He laughed, and Lizzie couldn't help but laugh with him. "I don't expect things to be the way they were between us before Lizzie, but I hope we can be friends."

"I'd like that," Lizzie said smiling at him.

"Are you ready for that dance?" Drake asked as he led her to the dance floor.

SEVEN

Lizzie had mixed emotions about going back to Chicago. She was ready to see Rob, but she hated leaving her family again. She promised herself that she would come back before the wedding and bring Rob with her.

Her dad helped load her things in the car. They went back inside arm in arm to say goodbye.

"Don't forget to think about renovating my house. Call me a little more often will you?"

"I promise, Granny."

"You can call us more often too you know," her mother said.

"I will, Mama."

"Bring that young man with you next time you come. I want to meet him."

"I will, Daddy."

"Have a safe trip. Call us when you get home."

"I will. I'll see you soon. I love you."

Lizzie waved goodbye as she left the driveway. *I have so much to tell Rob. Why hasn't he called?* To take her mind off Rob, she thought about renovating her grandmother's house. She had some good ideas by the time she turned in her rental car and made her way to the gate for the flight to Chicago.

While waiting to get through security, Lizzie noticed she hadn't put her engagement ring back on. She fumbled in her purse and found the papers that Rob had wanted her to look over. She had forgotten all about them. She told herself she would look at them later. Finding her ring, she put it back on her finger and went through security.

It was late when Lizzie opened her apartment door. She didn't unpack. She had to be at work early in the morning. She called Rob, still no answer. She wondered again why he hadn't called her. She undressed and went to bed. Tomorrow would be a long day.

LIZZIE'S ALARM went off for the fourth time. She reached for the snooze button again and saw the time. She was going to be late. She jumped out of bed rushed to get dressed and out the door. She made it to work only five minutes late. She was still rushing when she realized she hadn't called Rob again. *I'll try to call him on my break and look over those papers.*

The morning went by so quickly that she didn't have to time to think about anything but work. Her lunch break finally arrived. Celia was already enjoying her lunch and watching her favorite daytime drama when Lizzie entered the break room.

"How was the vacation?"

"It was great. The wedding was beautiful, and the best part was that I spent lots of time with my family."

"That would be the worst part for me but..." Celia broke off and reached for the television remote.

"Lizzie, look!"

Lizzie looked at the TV and cried, "Rob!"

It was a breaking news report. An unidentified man had been

found three days earlier at the site of a one car accident. He had not yet regained consciousness. The police were asking for help to identify him.

Lizzie rushed to the phone to call the number that was at the bottom of the TV screen. She gave them her name, phone number, address, and place of employment.

"Can you tell me what happened?" she asked the officer at the other end of the line.

"It appears that he lost control of the car and drove through a guardrail into a deep ravine. He was thrown from the car, before it caught fire. The smoke attracted the attention of a passerby, or he might still be there. No identification was found at the scene. We believe it was burned in the car. A melted cell phone was found but nothing else." She was given instructions to go to the hospital and see if she could identify the man.

"I'm going to the hospital, Celia. I'll be back as soon as I can."

She called a cab rather than driving to the hospital. She was shaking so badly she was afraid to drive. She was filled with worry about his injuries and thankfulness that he was alive. She ran into the hospital, gave her name, and asked for John Doe's room. The police had called the hospital so that they would be expecting her. She was immediately directed to ICU.

When Lizzie got off the elevator, a woman and two children were waiting to get on. As the doors closed behind her, one of them asked the woman, "Is Daddy going to be okay?"

Lizzie didn't hear the reply as she hurried toward the nurse standing in the hallway. "I'm here to see John Doe," Lizzie told the nurse.

"The doctor is with him now. You can wait here if you'd like."

"How badly is he hurt?" Lizzie asked.

"He's in critical condition. He has a concussion, some broken bones, and internal injuries, but he's stable. The doctors are concerned that he is still unconscious." The nurse glanced toward the rooms, "You can go in now. His room is two doors down."

Lizzie slowly walked into the room and over to the bed. It was Rob. There was no doubt about it. She sat down in a chair near the bed and held his hand.

"Rob, can you hear me? It's Lizzie." Tears welled up in her eyes; she was so thankful he was alive.

She wiped a tear from her cheek and saw a photo on the bedside table. She stood up and went around the bed to have a closer look. She froze, her mind struggling to process what she saw.

"OH MY GOD!" Lizzie's knees buckled and she sank to the floor beside the bed. The nurse rushed in to see what was happening. She picked Lizzie up from the floor and helped her to a chair. She was cold; so very cold.

"Are you all right, honey?"

"Oh my God! Oh my God!" Lizzie was rocking back and forth trying to hold herself together with her arms crossed over her stomach.

"I'll be right back; you stay put."

The picture was a large photo of Rob's dead wife and daughters. She thought about the woman and children in the hallway. She had barely paid attention, then, but the child asked if daddy would be okay. It was a girl. They were both girls and the woman...

The nurse came back with a glass of water. "The doctor will be here in a minute. You just sit there and rest," she said as she pulled a blanket around Lizzie.

Lizzie sat in Rob's room staring at him and the photo. She slowly gained control of herself. When the nurse left the room for a few minutes to care for another patient, Lizzie took her engagement ring from her finger and placed it beside the picture. She passed the nurse in the hall as she left and said, "He isn't the man I thought he was." The nurse stared at her in confusion as Lizzie got into the elevator.

Lizzie arrived at the hotel to find Celia had been waiting for her.

"Was it Rob?"

"Yes."

"Well, how badly is he hurt? What happened?"

Lizzie repeated the information the police and the nurse had given her. "He's still unconscious. They don't know when or if he'll come out of it. I need to work to keep busy."

Celia smiled, gave her a hug, and said, "I understand. If you need a break or need to talk, just let me know."

With tears in her eyes, Lizzie said, "Thanks."

Lizzie was busy all afternoon. She didn't have time to think about anything else. When she returned to her apartment, she began to unpack. She found the papers that Rob had wanted her to look over. She thought about destroying them, but curiosity made her hesitate. She opened the manila envelope and pulled out a life insurance policy. The policy was for her, naming Rob as the beneficiary. There was a second policy for Rob, naming her as the beneficiary. Rob had already signed it. She suddenly remembered a conversation they had had one evening.

Rob had told her that he had lost everything he had paying for the funerals and burial of his family. He had life insurance for himself, but there was none for his wife and children. He wanted to give each other the gift of life insurance so that if something should happen they would both be protected.

He had lied about his family being killed. The life insurance conversation was obviously a lie as well. What had he been planning? If he was divorced, why lie about the deaths? If he was still married... Lizzie cringed at the thought. Was he planning to get a divorce without telling Lizzie that his family was still alive?

The thought of having been dating and engaged to a married man troubled Lizzie. She had never imagined she would be the other woman. She had been jilted because of another woman. She would never knowingly become involved with a married man.

Lizzie was hurt, but the emotion she felt most was anger. She was angry at Rob for the lies and angry at herself for believing him. Divorced or married, he had lied to her. He lied about things that were important. How many other lies had he told? She didn't want to be with someone she couldn't trust, and she certainly didn't want to continue a relationship with a married man. It was over. She had to pick up the pieces and move on.

Lizzie looked around her apartment. The boxes she had been collecting for moving were in the corner of the bedroom. She was supposed to have turned in her resignation and canceled her lease today. She was glad she hadn't or she would be jobless and homeless.

She finished unpacking and sat down to relax. Her anger was beginning to subside. Now she felt tired and empty. She thought about turning her grandmother's house into an inn. She took her notes from her purse and looked through them making a few changes. *This could really work. It's secluded enough to be a nice hideaway and close enough that it would only be a thirty minute drive from town.*

She made a few more notes and sketches. *Why not try it? I have no reason to stay here now.* Lizzie picked up her phone and called her grandmother.

"Hi, Granny."

"Hi, Lizzie. I guess you made it home safely."

"I'm sorry I didn't call. It was late when I got home. I've been thinking about the inn renovations. I think we can make it work. I'd like to do it."

"Oh that's wonderful! When do you want to get started?"

"I'll have to turn in my resignation and cancel my lease. I'll probably have to be here at least another two weeks. It will be mid-July or later before I can move."

"What about Rob?"

Lizzie wished her grandmother hadn't asked about him. "That's over. I discovered I wasn't the only woman in his life."

"I'm sorry to hear that, but I'm so excited that you're coming home."

"I am, too, Granny," Lizzie said truthfully. "I'll call when I know more about my timeline."

The conversation ended, and Lizzie leaned back in her chair. She was more excited than she had anticipated. Tomorrow she would begin making arrangements to return to her home beside Paradise Creek.

EIGHT

The Fletcher family farm was one square mile of land where wheat, alfalfa, and cattle were raised. Paradise Creek formed the northern boundary of the farm and curving to the south formed the eastern boundary. A bridge had been built across the creek connecting the roads on either side. The creek had little water most of the year and at times none at all. However, the little creek raged like a mighty river when heavy rains came. Occasionally, the water would be high enough to rush over the bridge preventing anyone from crossing until the flood subsided. The house now called the Paradise Creek Inn was situated one quarter mile from the creek and the bridge.

Renovations had taken nine months to complete. The inn opened for business April 4, 2011. It was hidden from view by trees that surrounded the property. Guests would ride for miles on dry dusty roads, across the creek, and through a stand of trees to find themselves in a plush green oasis.

The grounds of the inn were between four and five acres in size surrounded by evergreen trees that had been planted as a windbreak decades earlier. Oak trees, elm trees, and shrubbery had been planted over the years to shade the house before air-conditioning had been invented. The house faced west and the shade was still welcomed in the summer heat. Shrubs and flower beds were added to the landscape. New windows and siding had been part of the outdoor renovations. A curved driveway and a sign announcing the name of the inn were added to the front lawn.

At the back, a patio had been created for outdoor events that ran the length of the house. A free form swimming pool was at the northeast end of the patio. The pool was similar in shape to a figure eight, rounded at the deep end but squared at the shallow end. A hot tub was located in the curve nearest the house and a stone water fall in the other. The grounds were covered in plush green grass from the patio to the outer edges. Near the eastern edge, there was a pond large enough to accommodate paddle boats and stocked with fish should a guest be inclined to wet a hook.

The downstairs had been four rooms: kitchen, dining room, and two living areas. The living area on the north side of the house was converted into an office and living quarters for Lizzie. Outside the office door was a foyer with a counter and computer desk for checking guests in or out. The kitchen was remodeled and updated with ample pantry and storage space. The rest of the downstairs area was opened into one large room suitable for indoor events. On the north side of the room near the kitchen was a long bar with a granite counter top for food service. A big screen TV and media center was at the opposite side of the room suitable for watching any number of programs or presentations. Under the staircase, were shelves filled with books and movies for the guests to enjoy.

Where there had been six small bedrooms upstairs, there were now four spacious rooms equipped with satellite TV, a blue ray player, and private bath. Each room had a balcony where guests could relax and watch the sunrise or sunset depending upon which side of the house they were located.

Severe thunderstorms and tornadoes were frequent in that part of Texas. It was decided that the cellar should be updated so that guests would have a comfortable place to wait out a storm. The cellar door was at the south end of the house. At the top of the steps were a light switch and a rechargeable flashlight. The steps descended into a large room that extended under the house. The walls were finished and painted and the floor had been tiled. Ceiling fans and lights fixtures hung overhead. Flashlights, candles, matches, and oil lamps were placed within easy reach on shelves near the bottom of the stairs and around the room in case of power outage. Sofas lined the walls for comfortable seating. Extra chairs, cots, and a battery operated radio were in a cabinet at the end of the room.

It was now mid-February. The inn had been open for ten months and business had been sporadic at best. The occasional banquet, wedding, or anniversary party had kept them afloat, but there were few overnight guests. However, there were signs of improvement. An anniversary party had been booked for May, a wedding booked for every weekend in June, and two in July.

"The place looks beautiful, Lizzie. I hardly recognize it. You did a fantastic job."

"It does look nice doesn't it," Lizzie replied.

"Yes, it does. I think it's time for you to take a break now," said Granny.

Lizzie had been invited to take a trip to the east coast with Faith and some other friends. She had been working on renovations to the inn and getting it in shape since she had returned home.

Granny continued, "I didn't want you to kill yourself turning this old house into an inn. Go and have a good time with your friends. We can run this place while you're gone."

"There's still a lot to do, Granny. We have to get the word out about this place, or it won't survive."

"Take this trip, Lizzie. You deserve it. Take a box of business cards with you and hand them out to people you meet."

Lizzie grinned at her grandmother. "I can't argue with that. It's a great idea."

"It's settled then."

"I guess it is," Lizzie said and kissed her grandmother on the cheek. "I'll start packing."

Lizzie and Faith left three days later for their east coast vacation. James, Ellen, and Lois took turns staying at the inn during the day. Because there were no guests or events scheduled, they would close the inn in the evenings and have the calls forwarded to their house.

Lizzie had been away for two days when a man knocked on the door of the inn. Lois opened the door and invited him in.

"We don't normally get walk in business here. Would you like a room?"

"No, ma'am, I'm Greg Jenkins with the FBI," he said as he showed her his credentials. "I'd like to speak with Lizzie Fletcher."

"Lizzie isn't here. May I help you with something?" she asked apprehensive and curious.

"When are you expecting her back?"

"She's on a trip with some friends. She won't be back for a couple of weeks. I'm her grandmother, Lois Fletcher. What is this about?"

"I'm sorry. I'm not at liberty to say. I only have a few questions for Miss Fletcher. Please, tell her I was here and have her call this number when she returns," he said handing her his card.

"I'll tell her."

"Thank you, ma'am. Goodbye."

"Goodbye."

Lois was confused and worried. *Why would the FBI want to talk to Lizzie?* She told James and Ellen about the visitor that evening at dinner. They decided to wait until Lizzie returned to tell her about the agent's visit. It was probably nothing to worry about, and they didn't want to spoil her trip.

When Lizzie returned, her grandmother told her about the FBI agent. Lizzie had no idea what it was all about. She nervously dialed the number on the business card.

"May I speak with Greg Jenkins please?"

"May I have your name?"

"This is Lizzie Fletcher. I had a message to call him."

After what seemed an eternity on hold listening to recorded music, agent Jenkins answered.

"Jenkins."

"This is Lizzie Fletcher. I understand you have some questions for me."

"Hello, Miss Fletcher. Thank you for calling."

"What is this all about?"

"I have some questions about one of your acquaintances in Chicago. Will you be available on Wednesday afternoon?"

"Yes, I will. Who do you need to ask me about?"

"I'd rather not discuss it on the phone. Is two o'clock in the afternoon convenient?"

"Yes, that will be fine," Lizzie answered confused.

"Good. I'll be at the Paradise Creek Inn on Wednesday, March 7, 2012 at 2 p.m. Thank you for your cooperation."

"You're welcome," Lizzie hung up the phone bewildered. *Who could possibly be under investigation by the FBI?* She thought of everyone she knew while living in Chicago and couldn't think of any reason why anyone would be under investigation.

"We're going to be here with you Lizzie," her dad told her at dinner that evening.

"You don't have to do that Daddy. I know you're busy with the farm."

"The farm can wait. I don't think you should answer questions from the FBI without someone else there."

"Okay, if you insist. The truth is I'd like the support. I have no idea who or what he wants to ask me about?"

Promptly at 2 p.m. on Wednesday, March 7th, a knock sounded at the front door of the inn. James opened the door and invited the agent inside.

"I have an appointment to see Lizzie Fletcher."

"She's on the patio. Right this way," James said as he closed the front door and led the way.

Lizzie stood when the two men came outside. "I'm Lizzie Fletcher. Would you like glass of lemonade or iced tea?" she asked nervously.

"I'm Greg Jenkins with the FBI," he said showing her his credentials. He shook her hand and said, "Iced tea would be very nice. Thank you."

"I'll get it Lizzie," Ellen said.

They sat down and nervously waited for Ellen to bring the tea. When she returned, Agent Jenkins explained the reason for his visit.

"Miss Fletcher, we have been investigating someone that we believe is an acquaintance of yours. I'd like you to look at a photo and tell me if you know this person."

"All right," Lizzie replied.

Agent Jenkins took a folder from his briefcase. He removed a photograph and slid it across the table toward Lizzie. She picked it up and gasped as she looked at it.

"Do you know him?"

"Yes, I do," Lizzie said her eyes tearing.

"Who is he?"

"His name is Rob Banyon."

"Rob?" her family said in unison.

"What do you know about him?"

Lizzie told him all she knew about Rob except that she had been engaged to him and how it ended. Finally she asked, "What has Rob done?"

"All in good time, Miss Fletcher. I still have some questions for you. Do you know a woman by the name of Celia Elkins?"

"Yes, we worked together in Chicago. She's my friend," Lizzie answered more confused than ever.

"Miss Elkins tells me that you were engaged to Mr. Banyon. Is that true?"

Lizzie cringed as she heard her family shift in their chairs. "Yes, I was," she answered as a tear slid down her cheek.

"You were but not now?"

"That's right."

"Why did you break off the engagement, Miss Fletcher?"

Lizzie hesitated before saying, "I haven't told anyone about this, not even my family. Is it really necessary?"

"Yes, ma'am. I'll answer your questions when you've told me what I need to know."

Lizzie told all she knew about Rob's accident and her visit to the hospital. "I haven't thought about this since I moved here. Why is it important?"

"I have one more question for you, Miss Fletcher. Then, I'll tell you what this is all about. Did Mr. Banyon ever ask you to sign a life insurance policy naming him as the beneficiary?"

Lizzie's jaw dropped. After a moment, she recovered from the shock and said, "Yes, he did. I was supposed to have read through it and another one he had naming me as beneficiary while I was here for a wedding."

"Do you still have them?"

"No, I don't. I shredded them both after I saw him at the hospital."

"That's understandable but unfortunate. What was the value of the policy?"

"It was for two million dollars."

The agent raised his eyebrows.

"Will you please tell me what this is all about?" Lizzie pleaded.

Lizzie and her family sat dumbfounded as Agent Jenkins told them the reason for his visit. The police department ran the ad asking for help to identify Rob. They had many callers saying they knew him. That wasn't unusual in a situation like that, but what was unusual was that six of them had the same story. Since those calls came from three different states, the FBI was called in.

FBI agents visited each of the six callers, showed them the photograph of Rob, and asked for his name. They all knew him, but all had different names for him. The first name was always Rob or Robert. The sir name started with a B each time, but the similarity ended there. The man in the photo was identified by all six as the husband of a friend who had moved to New York soon after the wedding. Two of the women that agents talked with had wedding photos. There was no doubt that the groom and the man in this photo were the same man. The first caller agents spoke with said that the man in the photo was widowed. He had apparently shown the bride the same picture and told her the same story. Others were asked if he was widowed. Some said yes. Some didn't know.

Agents in New York started trying to locate the brides. They found that each of them had died in an accident shortly after arriving in different cities around the state. The longest period of time was two months, the shortest one week. There were also calls from various insurance agents saying that the man had recently collected life insurance in amounts ranging from two hundred fifty thousand dollars to a million dollars. The names on those policies were checked. The names corresponded with the names of the dead brides and named Rob as beneficiary.

His fingerprints were not on file anywhere. We learned his name was Robert Berkett when a family member identified him. The FBI believed he used his business travels to cover his tracks with his family and his victims. He used his real name when he was at his home base or working. He used an alias when he met a woman with no nearby family and few friends. He would use the photo and the story about losing his family to win sympathy. He was probably emotional while he told the story. It helped him to earn each woman's trust. As far as could be determined, not one of the women or their friends sensed any danger. He was very convincing as a grieving family man ready to move on with his life.

"We believe you were to be his next victim, Miss Fletcher,"

Agent Jenkins said. "He was probably setting up your accident when he was in an accident himself. No identification was found on him. The car was rented under another alias. The photo that he showed you of his family was real. As you already know, they are still alive. What you may not know is that Berkett and his wife, Cindy, are still married with a residence in Manhattan. Apparently Berkett was supporting an expensive lifestyle with the life insurance money. We found where he had put away some of the money for college tuition for his daughters."

Lizzie was speechless. She couldn't imagine that the man she knew as Rob Banyon would be capable of killing anyone. The fact that he had already killed six women and that she was to be the seventh shook her to the core.

"Where is this man now? Is Lizzie still in danger?" James asked. He was angry and afraid.

"Berkett is still in a coma. His assets have been frozen while we are investigating. Miss Fletcher is in no danger from him at this time. If he regains consciousness, we may need to consider witness protection."

"Does his wife know?" Lizzie asked. She had always wondered if she knew or suspected that Rob had been claiming she was dead.

"We aren't sure how much she knows. At the moment it appears that she was not involved. We're still investigating that possibility. She believes we are investigating her husband's connection to six deaths, nothing more."

"Is there anything we need to do here to protect Lizzie?" Ellen asked her voice shaking.

"As long as Berkett is in the hospital, Miss Fletcher is safe. She would only be in danger if Cindy Berkett is involved. We don't believe she is or that she knows anything about Miss Fletcher."

"Will you let us know if Berkett's status changes?" James asked.

"Yes, sir. I'll keep you informed."

"Thank you."

"I have no more questions for you at the moment. Do you have any more for me?"

Lizzie couldn't think of anything else to ask. She was still processing how close she had come to death. She shook her head. James and Ellen said no in unison.

"Young man, what if the wife does know or finds out that her husband was involved with Lizzie and comes looking for her?" Granny asked.

Agent Jenkins paused for a moment, "I can tell you that Miss Fletcher won't be easy to find without help from a number of resources. If Mrs. Berkett should find this place, Miss Fletcher knows what she looks like."

Lizzie nodded and hugged her grandmother, "Rob must have lied to her, too. If she wasn't a part of it, she probably will never know about me."

"If there's nothing else, I'll be going. May I have your phone number so that I can stay in contact with you?"

Lizzie gave him her cell phone number and the number to the inn. James gave him his number also.

"I'll keep in touch. Please, call me if anything comes up or you remember anything else. Have a pleasant afternoon."

After Agent Jenkins had gone the questions from her family began. "Lizzie, why didn't you tell us about Rob?"

"You were engaged? Why on earth didn't you tell us?"

"Did you have any idea what was going on?"

"I didn't tell you before because he asked me not to tell you. He said he wanted to ask permission to marry me. I had no idea his family was still alive until that day at the hospital. I didn't know if he was still married or divorced. I was too ashamed and embarrassed to tell you I had been engaged to a man who might still be married. I didn't know how many other lies he had told me. I'm sorry I didn't tell you the whole story. I'm just as surprised as you are about the other women and their deaths."

Her parents still weren't satisfied but dropped the subject. Granny wasn't satisfied that Lizzie was safe. She wanted to find a way to protect Lizzie. After several scenarios were discussed, she agreed to drop the subject at least for the time being.

Lizzie made them all a nice dinner, and they watched a movie together before her family reluctantly went home for the night. Her dad made sure every door and window of the house was locked before getting into his truck and driving away.

TWO WEEKS WENT BY. No strangers came to the inn. No one came to the inn at all except Dan Hayes. Lizzie's dad had hired Dan to work on the farm and take care of the grounds at the inn. He also did odd jobs. Lizzie suspected he was really hired to keep an eye on her while her parents and grandmother were away. She wouldn't argue about it if it made her family feel better. There were times when the extra help was needed, and Lizzie had always liked Dan. He had been a year ahead of her in high school, and they had always gotten along well. Dan had worked at the inn almost two weeks when he mentioned his wife would be bringing him to work on Friday. Her car was going to be in the shop, and she needed his truck. He wanted Lizzie to meet her.

Friday morning Lizzie walked out onto the front porch to meet Dan's wife. She couldn't believe her eyes when she saw Megan Ford slide out of the truck.

"Lizzie, I'd like you to meet my wife, Megan."

"Well, well, well. If it isn't the fabulous Lizzie Fletcher," Megan said. Lizzie could almost see the sarcasm dripping from her lips.

"Hi, Megan," Lizzie said trying to be friendly.

"I guess you two have already met," Dan said confused.

"Of course we have, darling. We went to college together before she stole my fiancé."

Now, it was Lizzie's turn to be confused. "What are you talking about?" she asked Megan.

"Don't pretend that Drake didn't leave me and run straight to you."

"I've seen Drake once since I moved to Chicago. That was here at my cousin's wedding."

"If you think I believe that..."

"Megan, you're going to be late for work," Dan interrupted and pushed her into the truck.

As she drove away, Dan said, "I'm sorry about that. Sometimes she gets a little crazy."

"That's okay Dan, but I'd prefer not to see her again if she is going to behave like that. I'll be hiding inside when she comes to pick you up," Lizzie said with a grin.

"If she's still in that kind of a mood, I'll hide with you," Dan grinned back at her.

"How long have you been married?" Lizzie asked.

"Almost three years. If the inn isn't booked, would it be possible to have a birthday party here?"

"When would you like to have it?"

"Megan's birthday is April 11th, but we'll both be working that day. Would Saturday the fourteenth be okay?"

"I don't have anything booked for April, so it will be no problem. What sort of party would you like?"

"I thought we could have a nice dinner on the patio with family and a few friends. We could have some music and maybe dancing."

"That sounds nice. Do you want a formal, semi-formal, or casual party?" Lizzie kept asking questions, and before Dan realized it, the birthday party was planned.

"We have a semi-formal birthday party with dinner and dancing on the patio booked for April 14th for Dan and Megan."

"Will this be uncomfortable for you?" Dan asked apprehensively.

"Maybe a little, but it will be fine. Don't worry about a thing," Lizzie replied.

"I've heard the gossip about Megan and Drake. I didn't realize you were the fiancé thief," Dan teased. "I've heard her version. Someday, I'd like to hear your side of the story."

"Dan, it was a long time ago. We've all moved on." Seeing the disappointed look on his face, she continued, "But if it's important to you, I tell you about it one day."

"Thank you. It might help me figure out why she can't let it go."

Megan came to get Dan later than evening. True to her word, Lizzie stayed inside. She made a list of items she would need to purchase for the birthday party, watched a movie on satellite pay per view, and then went to bed. She had a full day ahead of her the next day.

NINE

Lizzie woke early the next morning to drive her parents and grandmother to the airport in Dallas. They were flying to Hawaii for an eleven day Hawaiian cruise. She was scheduled to pick them up at the airport on April 15. Lizzie would have only Dan for company until they returned. She hugged her family goodbye at the airport and started the drive home. She stopped in Vernon at one of the local supermarkets to stock up on supplies and purchase items needed for Dan's party. She picked up her dad's suit at the dry cleaners and drove home.

Clouds were starting to build in the southwest when she arrived back at the inn. She turned the TV on to the local weather, hung the suit in a closet upstairs, and put away the groceries. The phone rang just as she walked out of the pantry. Another couple wanted to book their wedding. Maybe things were finally picking up.

A loud annoying sound came from the television that Lizzie recognized as a severe weather alert. She sat down in front of the TV to see what was happening. The local station announced that a severe thunderstorm warning had been issued for Foard County. She was only a stone's throw from Foard County, so she paid close attention.

The inn would be in the path of the storm if it continued on its present course. She went outside to see a menacing cloud in the sky. She would have to stay on her toes until the storm was over. She went back inside and began gathering water and snacks to take to the cellar. She took fresh batteries for the radio and the flashlights. She might have to stay down there for a while, and she wanted to be comfortable.

It was getting dark outside, too dark for six in the evening. Thunder rumbled as she went back inside for a pillow and a blanket. Another alert sounded on the TV. A tornado warning had been issued. Radar indicated a tornado that appeared to be heading her way.

Lizzie ran out to the cellar. It was starting to rain, and she could hear a loud hum. It sounded like a small airplane. She had experienced enough to know that tornadoes didn't sound like airplanes. As that thought passed through her mind, a twin engine plane flew low over the roof of the inn. The little plane crashed simultaneously with a flash of lightening and a clash of thunder. It appeared to have gone down in the east pasture.

Lizzie threw the pillow and blanket into the cellar and ran to her Jeep Wrangler, cursing herself for not putting the top on. She climbed in and drove toward the crash. It was raining harder, and she was soaked to the skin by the time she reached the plane. It had crashed at the edge of the east pasture with one wing tipped into the creek bed. The pilot was struggling to get out. Lizzie stood on the brake, jumped out of the jeep, and rushed to help him out of the plane.

He had a nasty cut about his left eye, and his face was covered with blood. Struggling, Lizzie got him into the jeep. Lighting flashed, thunder rumbled, and the pilot shouted, "WHAT IS THAT?"

Lizzie turned to see a tornado dropping toward the ground and headed in their direction. She wasted no time answering him, ran to the driver's side of the jeep and jumped in. "HANG ON!" she shouted and gunned the motor. Hail stung them as they drove toward the house. Lizzie was praying they would reach the cellar in time and drove across the grounds right up to the cellar door.

She jumped out of the jeep running to the passenger side to help the injured pilot. They made their way through the cellar door and down the steps. The pilot collapsed on one of the sofas. Lizzie went back up the steps to close the cellar door as another flash of lightening revealed angry swirling clouds above.

Slamming the cellar door, she went back down the steps saying a silent prayer. Lizzie found the radio and turned it on. Locating a flashlight, she sat down to listen to the weather report. The radio crackled while rain and hail drummed on the cellar door. "It's probably not as big as it sounds," she said as much to herself as the man on the sofa. The radio crackled again and another weather alert was announced. Western Wilbarger County was now included in the tornado warning. "Well, duh. I could have told you that," Lizzie said to the radio.

A low moan came from the sofa. Lizzie looked closer at the injured pilot. She found a clean cloth and used some of the water she had brought down to clean his face. He had several cuts. The worst was above his left eye. The bleeding had stopped, but his face was beginning to look puffy. He had a large bump on the left side of his head. She felt his arms and legs for broken bones, but they seemed to be okay. She had no idea what other injuries he might have.

The roar above her head terrified her. "Now, that sounds like a train," she said aloud in an effort to calm herself. Suddenly the lights went out. She could no longer hear the radio. Still, she kept listening for the sounds of splintering wood and breaking glass. All she could hear was the roar above her and the hail pounding on the cellar door.

Lizzie said another silent prayer for the injured man and her inn. She was soaked to the skin and realized the pilot was too. Using the flashlight, she found the pillow and blanket she had tossed into the cellar. She covered the injured man, and tried to make him comfortable. She sat down on a sofa nearby to wait.

Eventually, the storm weakened. The only sounds to be heard in the cellar were the soft snores of two sleeping people. A weather alert on the radio startled Lizzie from her slumber. She was confused and unsure where she was. After a few moments, she was fully awake and recalled her situation. She used the flashlight and tried the light switch. There was still no power. She went back and checked on the pilot. He seemed to be resting comfortably, but she was concerned about the bump on his head. She was sure that some of the cuts needed stitches.

Lizzie made her way up the steps and opened the cellar door. It was too dark to see how much damage there may have been. At least the old house was still standing. She silently said a prayer of thanksgiving as she made her way into the house. She needed to get help for the man in the cellar. She tried using the inn's landline to call for help. The phone was dead. She tried her cell phone. No signal. The emergency radio in her office was battery operated, but she still couldn't reach anyone.

She went to her room and changed into dry clothes. She grabbed another pillow and blanket before going back to the cellar. She wanted to keep an eye on the injured man. She would spend the night in the cellar, because she couldn't get him up the stairs alone.

Lizzie woke to a beautiful morning. The sun was shining, birds were singing, and the air was cooled by the rain that had fallen during the night. She walked around the house surveying the damage and trying to get a signal on her cell. The satellite dish was gone along with the antenna for the emergency radio. A window on the west side of the house was broken and some shingles were missing from the roof. She went inside to try the office phone. It was still dead. She went upstairs to check the guest rooms. The floor was wet in one room near the broken window. Everything else seemed to be in good shape. The tornado had skipped over the inn.

Lizzie sat down to evaluate her situation. She had an injured man in the cellar needing medical attention. She had no power, no phone, and no emergency radio. The storm had probably downed power and phone lines. It was likely that the cell towers were damaged as well. How was she going to get help? The man was still unconscious and too heavy for her to move alone.

She went back to the cellar to check on the pilot. He was sleeping peacefully. She stared at him a moment. She smiled when she remembered the plane. Maybe the radio still worked. Lizzie's heart leapt with hope. She went up the steps and got into the jeep. The jeep made sounds of protest as she turned the key. *Come on*, Lizzie silently pleaded. "Yes!" she shouted when it finally started, and she raced to the east pasture where the plane had crashed.

Lizzie's brief moment of hope quickly faded. The plane was gone. *Where is it? It was right here.* "I know it wasn't a dream because the pilot is in my cellar," she said aloud. She got out of the jeep and walked toward the creek. It was running high with rushing water. There was evidence on the ground that the plane had been there. She had no way of knowing if it had been washed downstream or carried away by the tornado.

Lizzie got back into the jeep, and drove toward the bridge. Maybe she could drive across to get help. The creek was swollen outside its banks. The torrential rainfall had turned a virtually dry creek into raging rapids. All she could see was rushing water where the bridge was supposed to be. She sat staring at the creek. She had never seen it like this. She felt lost, and completely cut off from the rest of the world. She wondered how she could possibly get help now. She had no way to communicate with anyone and she was unable to cross the creek. It might take days for the water to subside, and she was sure the man in the cellar needed help right away.

Suddenly, she backed up. She turned the jeep around, and raced back to the inn. She stopped near the cellar door, and ran down the steps. She checked on the injured pilot before picking up the blanket that she had been using. She ran back up the steps and into the house. She gathered every sheet, blanket, and towel she could find. She pulled them off beds and out of storage. She took them out to the back lawn away from the trees and began to form them into a pattern. She looked at her watch and told herself she just might make it if they were flying today.

Finally, finished and exhausted, she went down into the cellar to check on her guest. She sat down and opened a bottle of water. If this didn't work, she didn't know what she would do.

Like clockwork, planes from Sheppard Air Force Base flew over the farm and the inn on training missions during the week. Lizzie was praying someone would be flying today. If not, no one would see her message until tomorrow.

Lizzie waited quietly in the cellar, monitoring her patient. She fell asleep after a while and didn't hear the crop duster flying over the inn. The pilot saw the S.O.S. that she had made on the lawn. He radioed for help as he continued his flight along the path of the tornado.

A short time later, Lizzie was awakened by a loud noise. She climbed out of the cellar to see a helicopter landing at the north east corner of the grounds. She ran over to meet the three men stepping out. She was so glad to see Dr. Hughes that she nearly knocked him off his feet when she ran to hug him.

"Hold on, hold on. You'll knock me over. What's the problem here?" he asked as they walked away from the chopper. The other two men followed them.

"I have an injured man in my cellar. I'm so glad someone saw my signal." Lizzie told the men what had happened and why she had to resort to such a crude signal for help. As they hurried to the cellar, the doctor made introductions. I believe you've already met our chopper pilot Martin Thomas. This is Sheriff Wade Adams. Both men nodded as she said hello."

"Dan Hayes was in my office trying to convince me to help him get across the creek when we got the alert from a crop duster," the sheriff told Lizzie. "The pilot had seen your S.O.S. and contacted us."

"Dan wanted to come with us, but there wasn't enough room in the chopper," Martin told her. "I sent word that you appeared to be okay when we saw you coming this way."

"Poor Dan. He was probably frantic," Lizzie said as she led them to the cellar.

"Do you have more flashlights down here Lizzie?" the doctor asked.

Lizzie hurried to get them from the storage cabinet. "Here they are. Where do you need them?"

"If each of you will shine one on the patient, I'll see what I can do for him."

The doctor examined the man for several minutes. "Some of those cuts are going to need stitches. Can we move him into the house where I can get a better look at him?"

"You can move him to my room. I don't have any power, but there should be enough light from my window at this time of day."

"All right boys, let's get him onto the backboard and into the house."

Sheriff Adams and Martin Thomas, with the help of the doctor, managed to get the man into Lizzie's room.

"Dr. Hughes, wouldn't it be better to take him to the hospital?" Lizzie asked.

"Yes, it would; yes, it would," he replied distractedly as he stitched the largest cut. "Unfortunately, the west side of the hospital was damaged in the storm. Every window on the west side was knocked out by hail. The rooms on the east side are occupied with people who were injured. The staff is doing the best they can with a full house and no power. For now, he is in the best place available."

"Miss Fletcher, do you know who the man is?" the sheriff asked.

For the first time, Lizzie more than just glanced at the sheriff. She hesitated for a moment as she took in his features. He was at least six feet of lean muscle. His hair was dark blonde and curled a little around his ears and his shirt collar. His green eyes seemed to look right through her and stirred her soul. He had a warm friendly smile that chased away the chill she had had since the night before. "N...no, no I don't," she stammered.

"How did you get him here Lizzie?" Martin asked.

"He was conscious when I got to him. He was able to get into my jeep and the cellar with my help. He hasn't been awake since. I was so busy that I didn't think to look for identification."

"Let's see if we can wake him up," Dr. Hughes said as he pulled smelling salts from his bag.

The man began to cough and tried to sit up to get away from the smell. "What happened? Where am I?"

"According to Lizzie, you were in a plane that crashed on her property just before a tornado passed through here last night. She was kind enough to rescue you and bring you to her inn," Dr. Hughes explained.

"What's wrong with me? I can't see."

"You have a mild concussion and several cuts that have caused swelling around your eyes. Thrashing around isn't good for you. I suggest that you remain still as much as possible until the swelling has gone down. I'm Dr. Hughes."

"Thank you, Doctor."

"You're quite welcome, and this is Sheriff Adams whom I believe has some questions for you."

The sheriff shook the man's hand and said, "Sir, if you would tell us who you are, we'll try to contact your family to let them know you're safe as soon as possible."

"My name is Montgomery Powell, but my friends call me Monty."

"Montgomery Powell, the actor?" Martin asked in astonishment.

"I probably don't look much like an actor now," he said grinning and then winced in pain.

"Can you tell us about the crash Mr. Powell?" the sheriff asked.

"I was flying to Dallas when I was caught in the storm and blown off course. The next thing I knew, it felt like the bottom had dropped from under me, and the plane started down. I saw an open field and tried to land. I landed harder than anticipated. I banged my head on the door, and must have broken the window. I remember hearing glass breaking. After that, I couldn't see well enough to maneuver the plane. The plane is probably seriously damaged. It was at a bad angle when it finally stopped. I was trying to get out when a jeep came at me like a bat out of hell."

Lizzie blushed. The other three men grinned at her.

"That would have been me, Mr. Powell. My name is Lizzie Fletcher. You're at the Paradise Creek Inn. The plane rolled partially into the creek from what I could tell. One wing appeared to be in the creek last night. That would probably have caused the angle you were talking about."

"So the plane isn't hurt as badly as I thought. That's great. Would you mind taking a look at it, Sheriff, to see what damage there is?"

Sheriff Adams hesitated a moment and then said, "I would, but the plane is no longer there."

"What?"

"My guess is that the tornado carried the plane with it as it passed through."

Monty Powell was speechless. Finally, he said, "That's a pretty scary thought."

"Yes, it is."

"How long have I been here? What day is it?"

They all looked at each other. "You've been here since last night. It's April 1st," Lizzie said.

"Mr. Powell, your injuries are relatively minor. As I was telling Lizzie earlier, the hospital is filled to capacity. I think the best place for you to recover is right here. Lizzie will take good care of you. I'll come out here periodically to check on your progress. The swelling should go down in a day or two, and the stitches can be removed at the end of the week."

"Thank you, Doctor. Thank you, all."

"In the meantime, we need to get you into some dry clothes. Lizzie would you happen to have anything suitable here?"

"No, I don't. I'll go borrow some of dad's things."

Lizzie left her patient in the capable hands of Dr. Hughes and drove down the road to her parents' house. She returned a few minutes later with pajamas and two changes of clothes.

"Lizzie, if you'll step outside. I'll help Mr. Powell out of his wet clothes."

Lizzie went into the kitchen and offered the men some tea. When the doctor had finished, he came into the kitchen and helped himself to a glass. The sheriff went back to speak with the actor.

"I'll let you know as soon as I've contacted your family. Our power and phone lines are down, so it may be a few days," Sheriff Adams told him.

"That's fine with me. I was taking a vacation from them all when I crash landed here. I'm in no hurry for them to find me."

Lizzie walked with the three men back to the helicopter. When they reached the chopper, Dr. Hughes turned to her and said, "Martin and I will be out here again tomorrow, Lizzie. Keep your patient quiet and comfortable."

"Thank you for coming to help me. Please, tell the crop duster pilot how much I appreciate his help. Oh, and please, tell Dan that I'll be all right."

"We were glad to help," Sheriff Adams said as he shook her hand.

Lizzie felt a warm, tingling sensation as he held her hand just a little longer than was necessary. "Goodbye and thank you again," she said.

The sheriff tipped his cowboy hat and climbed in the chopper.

Lizzie walked back toward the inn and sighed with relief as the helicopter carrying the three men flew back toward town. She said a prayer of thankfulness that her guest was not seriously injured.

Lizzie went back inside to see if her patient needed anything. "Would you like something to eat or drink?" she asked.

"I'm a little thirsty."

"I have lemonade, tea, and water. I don't know how cold it will be since the power is off."

"Water will be great. Thank you, Miss Fletcher."

"Please, call me Lizzie."

"I will if you'll call me Monty."

"It's a deal," she said and left the room to get a bottle of water.

When she returned, Monty was sleeping. She gently placed the bottle on the nightstand and left the room.

It was late afternoon when Lizzie went outside to collect the sheets, towels, and blankets she had used and carried them inside. She went upstairs to clean up the broken glass in the guestroom and wiped up the water from the floor with towels. Her next stop was the storage shed where she found a ladder, hammer, nails, and a piece of wood. She took the ladder and the other items to the west side of the house. She climbed the ladder to the broken second floor window and boarded it up.

While she was on the ladder, she had a better look at the roof. Some shingles were missing. Others were damaged, but she didn't think the entire roof would need replacing. She would have someone come look at it when she could. Lizzie put the ladder and tools back in the shed and checked the rest of the house for damage.

She would have to call the satellite company to replace the satellite dish, and a new antenna for the emergency radio would have to be purchased. Lizzie searched the grounds for the satellite dish. She looked in the trees, the pool, and the pond. It was nowhere to be found.

The sun was beginning to sink on the horizon when Lizzie walked back to the house. Once inside, she lit candles and oil lamps to give her enough light to work by. She checked on her still sleeping guest then went to the office to make a bed on the sofa. She went to the bookshelf, chose a favorite book, and went back to the office. She opened the door between the office and her room so that she could hear if Monty should need anything.

Just as she was about to settle down with her book, she heard a noise from the next room. She got up to see what was happening.

"Can I help you, Monty?"

"I hate to ask, but would you mind leading me to the bathroom?"

Lizzie showed him the way to the adjoining bath and waited outside the door. "Is there anything I can get for you? Anything you need?"

"You wouldn't happen to have a sandwich and some pain pills would you? I'm getting hungry and have one hell of a headache."

"I think I can handle that. Dr. Hughes left something for your pain," she told him as she helped him back into bed. "I'll be right back."

When she returned, he ate hungrily, took the pills, and chugged the entire bottle of water. "Ah, thank you Lizzie. That was great."

"You're welcome. I'll be right next door, so call out if you need anything."

"That's a deal. Goodnight."

"Goodnight."

Lizzie was too tired now to read. She blew out the lamp and fell asleep as soon as her head hit the pillow.

TEN

After a full night of sound sleep, Lizzie woke refreshed Monday morning. She dressed quickly and checked on the still sleeping Monty. *Montgomery Powell is in my house. Who would ever believe it?* She was a big fan, and he starred in many of the movies she owned.

Montgomery Powell was an award winning actor. He was quite handsome and most often played the leading man. He had salt and pepper hair and eyes the color of warm milk chocolate. He had a charming smile that made his eyes twinkle while revealing perfectly straight, white teeth. He had a natural good humor and seemed to be at ease with everyone, especially the ladies.

Lizzie quickly took items from the refrigerator and closed the door. She checked the freezer to see if the food inside was thawing. *The power had better come back on soon*, she thought. She put together a few things for breakfast, placed it on a tray, and carried it into the room where Monty was resting. He was getting back into bed when Lizzie brought in the tray.

"I thought you might like some breakfast," Lizzie said as she placed the tray within his reach.

"Yes, I'm starving."

"I'm sorry it isn't a hot breakfast. Until the power comes back on, we'll have to eat cold meals."

"Any kind of meal is great. Thank you."

"Enjoy. If you need anything, give a shout. I'll be in the kitchen."

Monty ate greedily. Lizzie brought pain medication for him when she came for the breakfast tray. He was still sleeping when Dr. Hughes and Martin arrived.

"How is your patient today, Lizzie?"

"He's had a headache but is eating."

"I'll just go in and have a look."

Dr. Hughes returned to the kitchen when he had finished the examination. "I think he'll be fine, Lizzie. Try to get him up tomorrow and walk around the grounds. The fresh air should lift his spirits."

"Whatever you say, Doctor," Lizzie grinned at him.

"We saw a crew working on the power lines on our way here," Martin told her. "You should have power by this time tomorrow."

"Not a minute too soon. The food in my freezer is starting thaw. What does the creek look like?"

"I could see the bridge from the air. The water doesn't appear to be as swift as it was yesterday," Martin replied.

"Oh that's good news."

"We'll be back on Wednesday. Send up another S.O.S. if you need anything," Dr. Hughes told her.

"I hope it won't be necessary."

The two men waved goodbye and walked to the helicopter. Lizzie stood on the patio and watched it take off. She wanted to see the creek for herself. After finding Monty sound asleep, she drove to the bridge. *I might be able to drive across in a day or two*, she thought. She drove back to the inn feeling much better about her situation than she had the day before.

Lizzie spent the afternoon picking up shingles and broken tree limbs from the grounds of the inn. She would look in on Monty periodically and finding him asleep would continue working. When the sun began to set, she went back inside, lit the candles and lamps again and began to make dinner.

"Hello."

Lizzie jumped and said, "My goodness you startled me. I thought you were still sleeping."

"I'm sorry. I felt like moving around a bit. I could hear you and just followed the sound."

"There's a chair a couple of feet to your left if you'd like to sit down while I make us something to eat."

"Great, I'm starved. Tell me about yourself Lizzie."

"Okay, but only if you tell me about yourself."

"Oh, that could take all night," he laughed.

The two sat together eating a cold sandwich, drinking warm lemonade, and getting to know each other into the early hours of the morning. When they finally said goodnight, Lizzie felt she had a good friend.

Lizzie woke the following morning to the annoying white noise of a television with no reception in the outer room. Power had been restored. She checked the land line phone. It too had been restored. Her cell phone still didn't work, but progress was being made. Monty was still sleeping, so she drove to see if the flood waters had subsided. She was thrilled to find that the water was flowing under the bridge instead of across it. She drove back to the inn to phone her insurance agent, a roofer, and the satellite company. She had arranged for them to come out the following afternoon. Her next phone call was to Dr. Hughes to inform him that the creek bridge was now accessible.

Dan Hayes had also been waiting for the opportunity to cross the creek bridge. He had been unable to get to the farm to check on Lizzie. He had been pestering the sheriff asking for news. He was supposed to be watching over her and was frustrated that he couldn't get in touch with her or to the inn. He was relieved to learn that Lizzie and the inn were fine, but he still felt he needed to be there.

Dan arrived at the inn just as Lizzie started making breakfast. She asked if he would mind checking the rest of the family property while she cooked. He drove the half mile to the Fletcher's house and searched for damage. Then he checked the out buildings and drove around the farm. The only damage appeared to be at the inn. He was thankful it was minor. He went back and told Lizzie that everything was okay. She told him about the damage she had found. After breakfast, he would go into town for supplies and an antenna for the emergency radio. He hoped to finish the cleanup by the end of the work day.

One week later, the damaged shingles had been replaced and a new satellite dish was installed. Cell phones were working again. Monty's stitches had been removed, and he was at last recognizable. Sheriff Adams had gotten in touch with Monty's family. His girlfriend now phoned at least once a day. Lizzie thought he would probably go home soon. She had enjoyed his company and would miss him.

Monty told her that he liked being at the inn and asked Lizzie if he could book one of the guest rooms. He handed her his credit card and booked the room for a week. She was glad to have her own room back and that he would be staying for a while longer.

Megan's birthday party was only a few days away, and Lizzie was busy with preparations. She still had plenty of time, but with all that had been happening, she felt rushed. Monty offered to help. She hesitated but agreed. They had the inn decorated and the food prepared with little time to spare.

Before the party guests began to arrive, Monty said, "Lizzie, if you don't mind, I'd like to stay incognito a while longer. I'll just stay in my room this evening."

"I understand and thanks again for your help."

He winked at her as he went up to his room. She checked everything one more time before the guests began to arrive. It was as perfect as she could make it. Dan and Megan arrived first. They were both pleased with the décor and the food. Megan practically gushed. As more guests came, they were shown to the patio and seated for dinner.

Lizzie had hired some experienced waitresses for the event. As dinner was served, she mingled and chatted with the guests. She made sure everything went like clockwork. She breathed a sigh of relief as the dessert dishes were collected and the dance music began to play. Megan had been drinking heavily but had remained pleasant throughout dinner.

Suddenly, Megan stood up and walked toward Lizzie. "It wasn't enough that you had to steal my fiancé years ago. Now you're trying to steal my husband, too." She threw her glass of red wine at Lizzie. It ran down her face and neck onto her white dress.

Lizzie paused for a moment, embarrassed. Dan rushed to pull Megan away as Lizzie said, "If you'll excuse me ladies and gentlemen, it appears that I need to change. Please, enjoy yourselves, and I'll return shortly."

Lizzie was staring into her closet when Monty knocked on her door.

"May I be of assistance?" he asked.

"You saw that?"

"I did. It was completely uncalled for." He reached into her closet and pulled out a royal blue dress that she hadn't worn since she left Chicago. "I think you should wear this one. Would you happen to have a suit in my size hanging around somewhere?" he asked as she took the dress from him.

"One of dad's suits is in a closet upstairs."

"I'll go in search of Dad's suit and meet you back here."

Lizzie smiled as he left the room. She washed her face, reapplied her makeup, and wiggled into the dress. She was pleased to see that it still fit. She was looking in the mirror, repairing her hair when Monty returned.

He smiled when he saw her and said, "You look beautiful."

"Thank you! You look pretty good yourself," she said smiling back. "Are you sure you want the whole town to know that you're here?"

"I was getting tired of being incognito anyway," he shrugged and smiled. He offered her his arm, and they walked out to the patio together.

Everyone was dancing. They didn't notice the handsome couple right away. As Monty and Lizzie danced around the patio, she heard gasps and whispers.

"Is that who I think it is dancing with Lizzie? It can't be, but it certainly looks like him."

"Oh my! Is that Montgomery Powell?"

The song ended, and Lizzie looked around to find everyone had stopped dancing and was staring at her dance partner.

"Ladies and gentlemen, I'd like to introduce my friend Montgomery Powell."

Monty smiled at her, kissed her hand, and led her around the patio for another dance. The guests watched the pair dance for a moment and then joined in. Monty would wink at Lizzie periodically and cut in to dance with one of the older ladies. They beamed at him and giggled like school girls. Lizzie would dance with their husbands who were almost as pleased to be dancing with her.

Everyone was having a wonderful time. Everyone except the guest of honor and her husband. Megan was sulking at a table near the pool while Dan tried to convince her to dance with him. Giving up, he walked away and asked his sister to dance. Megan stood up and took a few drunken steps before deciding she had better sit down again. As she was sitting down, she leaned back too far. The chair and its occupant fell into the swimming pool.

Dan rushed over to help her out with Monty close behind. Lizzie went inside for towels and a blanket. Megan was furious when she was pulled from the pool. She was stomping, yelling, and flailing her arms when she accidentally knocked Dan and Monty into the pool.

Losing her balance, she fell in again. The two men in the pool began to laugh. The remainder of the guests watched for a moment and began to laugh with them. Lizzie offered the towels and blanket to Megan's mother. "I think she would much rather you helped her."

Roxanne Ford smiled gratefully at Lizzie, "You're probably right. I apologize for her behavior this evening." Lizzie smiled back at her as Roxanne turned to help her daughter.

The trio was helped from the pool, and the guests went home. It had been a success in spite of a few uncomfortable moments. Lizzie said goodnight to Monty and explained that she would be going to Dallas the next morning to pick up her family.

"Do you mind if I tag along? It's time I went home."

"Of course you can. I've enjoyed having you're here."

"I've enjoyed being here, and I plan to come back," he said and smiled.

"Tell all your friends," Lizzie laughed.

"You can count on it."

ELEVEN

Montgomery Powell would be flying back to Los Angeles after Lizzie's family landed at the Dallas airport. They had enjoyed the time together during the drive and didn't want it to end.

"Monty, will you have time to meet my family?" Lizzie asked as she parked the jeep.

"I'm sure I will. I have two hours before I can board," he said smiling that charming smile at her. The pair continued their conversation into the airport.

"Thanks for coming to my rescue last night," Lizzie said.

"It was my pleasure. I always like to dance with the prettiest girl in the room or in this case on the patio," he said grinning at her. "I was watching the party from the balcony because I was getting bored watching television. There was a news bulletin every half hour." He began to do his impression of a news anchor, "Breaking News! Actor Montgomery Powell has been found. We are told that he is recovering from minor injuries at an undisclosed location. Mr. Powell was reported missing two weeks ago when he failed to arrive at his destination. Family, friends, and fans feared the worst when a section of his plane was found in Oklahoma. Once again, actor Montgomery Powell is alive."

Lizzie laughed so hard her sides ached. "You do that so well," she said when she caught her breath.

"I heard what that woman said and saw her throw the wine in your face. I've never seen anyone do a better job of handling such a bad situation. I guess I'm a bit conceited, but I thought she'd realize you weren't interested in her husband if she saw you with me. You aren't interested in him are you?" he asked grinning at her inquiringly.

Lizzie smiled at him, "No, we're just friends. I don't date married men."

"You mean I'll have to wait until my divorce is final to ask you out!" He feigned heartbreak and winked at her.

Lizzie laughed. "I'll have to take a number by then I'm sure. I was proud to be seen with you last night. It didn't hurt that you stopped the gossip that Megan tried to start. I'm not sure it stopped Megan."

Lizzie waved at her family when she saw them coming her way.

"Lizzie!"

"Come meet my family, Monty."

Lizzie introduced Monty to her family. They exchanged pleasantries and hugs.

"You have quite a girl here. She saved my life," Monty told them.

They looked at Lizzie with pride and curiosity. "I'll tell you about it on the way home," Lizzie assured them.

"Uh oh. I've been spotted. It was nice to meet you, and I hope to see you again soon. Bye, Lizzie." Monty said as he kissed her on the check and ducked around the corner to avoid a group of female fans.

Lizzie waved at him and laughed. "He'll probably miss his flight if they catch him," she explained. She hugged them all again, and they left the airport happy to be together. Soon they were comfortably settled in the car and through the heaviest traffic.

Ellen said, "Okay Lizzie, talk."

"What do you want to talk about Mama?" Lizzie teased.

"She wants to talk about that handsome man you introduced us to, and so do I. He's more handsome in person than on the screen," Lois prodded.

"I want to hear how you saved his life and what was going on at the time," James added.

Lizzie told them everything that had happened while they were away. They were frightened when she told them about the tornado but were impressed with the way she handled the disaster.

"Monty told me on way to the airport that he'd like to make a movie at the inn. He needs to talk to some people about getting it started first. What do you think?"

James was the first to speak. "It would be great publicity for the inn."

"And we'd make a nice profit with movie people around," Ellen chimed in.

"If we'll see more of that handsome Montgomery Powell, I'm all for it," said Granny.

Lizzie laughed. "I want to hear about your cruise."

They took turns telling her about their vacation. James said that Granny had met an interesting man on the ship. She denied it and changed the subject.

Lizzie had closed the inn for the day. When she returned, the answering machine had thirty messages. Callers wanted to book parties, weddings, and weekend stays. Word must have spread that Monty had been staying at the inn. His kindness may have helped more than either of them realized.

Jotting down the names and numbers, she cleared the answering machine. She would return the calls tomorrow and hoped more would be coming. She looked around to see what needed to be done now and what could wait until morning. She decided it could all wait. She would have lots of help tomorrow, and she wanted to relax with a good book tonight. She went to the office to retrieve the book

DEATH ON PARADISE CREEK   101

she had left there. She got into her pajamas, plumped her pillows, and turned her bed down. After going to the kitchen for a snack, she settled down to read. She dozed off before she had finished the first chapter.

Dan was at the inn early Monday morning. "Lizzie, I want to apologize. I had no idea Megan would behave that way. I'm so sorry that she was so nasty and ruined your dress. Please add the cost of the dress to my bill," he said as he handed her a typed letter.

"Dan, there was no harm done. I was temporarily embarrassed, but that's all. Don't worry about my dress," she said.

Dan looked miserable as she opened the letter. "What's this?"

"I don't expect you to keep me on after what happened. It'll look better on my resume if you'll accept my resignation rather than fire me."

"Dan, you aren't going to be fired, and I don't want your resignation. You're a big help here, and you do great work."

He looked at her with amazement.

"However, I think that Megan should stay away from here unless it's absolutely necessary."

"You'll get no argument from me," Dan said relieved.

"Granny will be here soon to answer the phone. If you'll get started with the outdoor cleanup, I'll help you when she gets here."

Dan smiled and said, "Yes, ma'am." He walked out to the patio whistling as he went.

Lizzie joined him a short time later. As they cleaned the patio, Dan asked her again what had happened all those years ago. She told Dan the story about her breakup with Drake and what she had learned later. Dan listened without interrupting. He was silent for a long while after Lizzie finished her story.

"Megan's version of the story is different. She told me that she had been engaged to Drake and was pregnant with his baby when he met you and left her. There are some similarities in the story, but that is a big difference."

"I know. It's understandable that you want to believe your wife. Drake doesn't live here anymore, but his family does. Maybe you should talk with them."

"I've thought of talking to Roxanne about it. I don't know if she would tell me the truth."

"Megan and I were friends before this all happened, but we were never close. I don't know what happened to change things. I hadn't seen Megan since I moved to Chicago. Whatever this is about, I hope the situation improves for the two of you."

"That makes two of us," he sighed as he filled another trash bag with party debris.

They finished cleaning the grounds, and Lizzie went inside to finish her indoor chores. She was taking linens from the dryer when Granny asked her to come to the office.

"I've returned all of these calls, and we're booked until October. Calls are still coming in. Everyone hopes to get a glimpse of Montgomery Powell. Some didn't want to make a reservation. They only wanted to know if he was still here."

"We'll probably have some cancellations when they find out that he left yesterday."

"We probably will, but hopefully not too many."

The phone rang, and Lois was busy again.

Lizzie finished the laundry and made lunch. When they had finished eating, Dan went to the east pasture to mend the fence where Monty's plane had crashed. Granny went back to the phone and Lizzie continued her work inside.

Suddenly, Dan burst through the door, "Lizzie, you have to see this. We have to call the sheriff."

"What's wrong?"

"One of the fence poles rolled down into the creek. I went to get it and saw... Come with me and bring your cell. You have to see this! We have to call the sheriff!"

Dan was muddy, pale, and shaking uncontrollably. Lizzie got into his truck and rode with him to the east pasture. She hung on for dear life as Dan sped toward the creek. He slammed on the brakes and jumped out of the truck. He practically pushed her into the creek bed.

"Look down there. Do you see it? Is that what I think it is?"

Lizzie slid in the mud as she climbed down for a closer look. Now she understood why Dan was so upset. She wasn't feeling very calm herself. Trembling, she climbed the bank and managed to dial 911.

"Would you send the sheriff out to the Paradise Creek Inn as soon as possible? No, it isn't a life threatening emergency. Yes, I understand, but I don't happen to have that number. She listened for a moment. "Fine, tell him that we believe we've found a man's foot. Yes, please ask him to call me at this number." She gave her cell phone number to the dispatcher.

Lizzie hung up and looked at Dan, "She'll have him call me." They sat on the tailgate of his truck lost in their own thoughts waiting for the sheriff's call. Lizzie's cell rang, startling them both.

"Hello. Yes, Dan Hayes found what appears to be a man's foot. No, it has probably been here for some time. It's sticking out of the creek bank about five feet from the surface. It looks like an old boot that has partially rotted away with bones inside. Okay, see you then."

Dan looked at Lizzie, "Well?"

"He says he'll be here with a crew in an hour. He wants one of us to meet him at the house and the other to stay here."

"Why?" Dan asked.

"He doesn't want the scene to be disturbed any further."

"Who's going to disturb it? No one else knows about it."

"I don't know."

They sat on the tailgate in silence for a moment. Finally, Dan said, "This is pretty weird."

"It sure is."

They were silent for a moment longer. Lizzie finally said, "Dan, you should go to the house to clean up and then come relieve me in thirty minutes. That way neither of us is stuck out here very long."

"Thanks, Lizzie. I'm a little shook up."

Dan drove back to the house while Lizzie sat in the shade of a tree on the edge of the creek bank. She was trying to calm down and picking at the red mud on her jeans. She couldn't help but wonder about the owner of the foot. *Who could it be? It looked like a man's boot. How long has he been buried there? Did he die of natural causes or was it murder?* She tried to imagine what sort of person he had been.

She heard the truck coming back and looked at her watch. She had been lost in thought and hadn't been aware of the time. Dan got out of the truck and handed Lizzie the keys.

"Lois is asking a lot of questions. I didn't answer. I thought I'd leave that to you."

"Okay, thanks, Dan. Are you feeling better?"

"I think so. I'll been fine until the sheriff gets here."

Lizzie got into his truck and drove back to the house. Her grandmother met her at the door.

"What's going on, Lizzie? Dan looks like he's seen a ghost. He wouldn't tell me a thing."

"He's pretty shaken up, Granny. He found something that looks like a man's foot. The sheriff should be here soon."

"Do you think it is a foot?" she gulped.

"It looks that way to me. Will you call Daddy and tell him what's happening? He'll probably want to be here when the sheriff arrives. I'm going to get some of this mud off."

"I'll do it right now," Lois said as she walked to the office to make the call.

Lizzie cleaned up, made herself a glass of lemonade, and sat down to wait for the sheriff. James was the first to arrive. Ellen came in shortly after. Lizzie told them what she had told the sheriff while they waited.

After what seemed to be an eternity, Sheriff Wade Adams arrived with his team. Lizzie led them to the east pasture. Dan was visibly relieved when he saw them. "Mr. Hayes, would you mind showing us what you've found?" Sheriff Adams asked.

Dan led them into the creek and pointed at the foot sticking through the bank. The team examined it and concluded that it was indeed a human foot.

"We're going to start digging the body out. Please, don't tell anyone about this. We don't need any sightseers out here in our way."

"We won't, Sheriff. We'd rather not have uninvited guests out here either."

"We'll probably work until we get him out of there. It's possible that we could be here all night. At least the ground is still soft from the recent rains."

"I'll come back in an hour or two with some cold drinks."

"We'd appreciate that, Miss Fletcher," the sheriff said as he smiled at her.

Dan and Lizzie went back to the inn. Lizzie told her folks what the sheriff had said.

An hour and a half had passed when Lizzie drove out to the east pasture with large jugs of lemonade and iced tea. The men were hot and tired. They sat on the truck tailgates and on the ground resting while they guzzled the cold drinks.

Sheriff Adams took Lizzie by the elbow. The touch of his hand sent a warm tingling sensation up her spine. He led her around the dig site. A tarp had been laid on the ground where remains were to be placed as they were unearthed.

"It looks like he's been here a very long time," he told Lizzie. "When the creek flooded, the water eroded the bank and exposed part of the remains. Would you like to see what we've found so far?"

"Yes, I've been wondering what's happening out here. Do you have any idea who it might be?"

"Not yet," the sheriff said smiling at her.

"Sheriff, you'd better have a look at this." One of the team members handed him an old piece of leather. He looked at it closely.

"What does that look like to you, Miss Fletcher?"

Lizzie examined the leather carefully before answering. "It looks like a key ring with some keys on it."

"That's what I thought, too."

"What do you think it is?"

"We won't know for sure until we've finished running the forensic tests. It looks like an old piece of hand tooled leather."

After a few minutes he asked, "Miss Fletcher would it be possible to order sandwiches for my men? If you'll keep a tab for us, I'll make sure your reimbursed," he said touching her hand as he took the leather from her.

"I...I'd be happy to," she stammered. "My dad will probably want to come out here to see what's happening."

"That'll be okay. He may be able to answer any questions that come up. I'll send the crew to the inn in shifts if that's okay."

"That'll work. I'll tell Daddy he can watch while you dig."

Lizzie went back to the house. She told her dad that he could go to the site. He hurried out the door while she told her mom and granny what had been found.

Lois wasn't happy. "Who would have buried someone on my land?"

"I wonder who the poor man was," Ellen said.

"The sheriff said it may take a long time to find out," Lizzie told them.

They discussed who it might be and why the man was buried there while they made sandwiches and more cold drinks for the men. Lizzie wanted to be out there watching what was happening. After the sandwiches were made, she went to look at the list of parties and weddings that had been booked. Every weekend was booked with an event, but the guest rooms were still available. Wishing she could be outside watching the dig, she wandered around the inn restlessly.

The crew from the dig began coming to the inn in groups of three. They enjoyed the air conditioning as they relaxed and joked while they ate. Sheriff Adams came in with the last group. "You don't know how much we appreciate the food and drinks ladies. Miss Fletcher may get a marriage proposal or two."

Lizzie blushed. "It's what we do. We like for our guests, or those working near, to feel welcome and comfortable."

"We certainly feel welcome. That's unusual for those of us in law enforcement. I'll have a hard time getting them to leave."

"I'm glad they feel comfortable here."

"There will be a generator truck coming out here before it gets dark. We'll be setting up lights so that we can dig through the night. I'd appreciate it if you would show them the way out there, Miss Fletcher."

"Certainly, Sheriff. You'll probably be ready for something cold to drink by the then."

"I've already mentioned this to James, but I would like y'all to call me Wade. We'll probably be seeing a lot of each other before this is all over."

"I'm Ellen."

"I'm Lois, or you can call me Granny."

"You can call me Lizzie."

Lizzie's dad came in to the kitchen, "Wade, they've found another body."

"I'd better get back to the site. Thank you, ladies." He smiled at Lizzie then left the room.

The generator truck arrived an hour later, and Lizzie led them to the site. She had a case of cold bottled water to give the men. Wade smiled, and she felt that warm tingling sensation again as he took her elbow while leading her to see the new finds.

"Sheriff, we've found something else."

"Excuse me, Lizzie."

Lizzie remained where she was and waited for the sheriff. He returned with another piece of old leather. He handed it to Lizzie. There were letters on this piece. The bottom of one letter was missing, but it appeared to be an E or F. The other was clearly a K.

Lizzie looked into the sheriff's eyes. Somehow he made her feel he could read her thoughts. That idea gave her a strange feeling in her stomach. She tried to recover by looking back at the piece of leather before asking, "Is it part of the other piece, Wade?"

"I don't think so. It was found near the second body. We should be finished here before sunrise. We'll need to keep the area covered and roped off until we're certain we have everything. It will take several months for the forensic tests to be completed."

Lizzie went back to the inn. Her family didn't want to miss anything, so they decided to stay at the inn a while longer. The four were watching a movie together when the phone rang.

"Thank you for calling Paradise Creek Inn. How may I help you?" Lizzie answered.

"May I speak with Miss Lizzie Fletcher, please?"

"This is Lizzie."

"Good evening, Miss Fletcher. This is Agent Greg Jenkins."

"Hello, Agent Jenkins. How are you?"

"Fine, ma'am. Thank you. I have an update for you. Robert Beckett passed away yesterday afternoon. We believe that you are no longer in danger."

"Is his wife still under investigation?"

"No, ma'am. We found no evidence linking her to the murders. We believe she had no knowledge of her husband's activities."

"Thank you for calling!"

"My pleasure. Goodbye"

"Goodbye."

"Daddy, guess what?"

James had just walked out onto the front porch and was about to close the door. "What?"

"That was Agent Jenkins. I'm no longer in danger."

"What changed?"

"Rob passed away yesterday afternoon. They believe his wife knew nothing about it."

"What a relief."

"We can still keep Dan around can't we? He's a great worker."

James smiled at his daughter, "I know he is. That was the main reason I hired him. Keeping an eye on you was extra duty. You'd better tell your mother and grandmother the news." He went back outside and sat in one of the rocking chairs on the porch. He liked to be alone when he had a lot to think about.

Lizzie told Ellen and Granny about the phone call. They both cried with relief. She hadn't realized how worried they had been. She had been too busy to think about the danger.

Just before three in the morning, Wade knocked on the back door of the inn. Lizzie had fallen asleep on a sofa after her family had gone home.

"Hi, Wade. How is it going out there?"

"I'm sorry I woke you, Lizzie. I came to tell you that we've finished. We'll be packed up and out of your way soon. Do you happen to have the total for what we owe you?"

"I can have it for you in a few minutes. Please, come in." Lizzie quickly calculated the bill and gave it to the sheriff.

"Thank you. We're going to cover the dig site and rope it off for a few days. I'll send some men to fill in the hole when I'm sure we've recovered everything we can."

"I'd appreciate that. I'm sure Dan will too." Lizzie said with a laugh.

"I'll let you get some sleep. Thanks again for your help today. I'll probably be back out sometime tomorrow for another look around. Goodnight, Lizzie."

"Goodnight, Wade."

The following morning, Lizzie was busy making decorations for

Saturday's anniversary party. There were finished decorations and supplies to make more spread all around the banquet room.

"Lizzie, you have a visitor." Ellen grinned as Jan walked into the room.

"Jan! I wasn't expecting to see you before Saturday," Lizzie said as she hugged her cousin.

"I know, but I decided to bring these photos of Eli's parents for the party. Besides I wanted to see you without all those people around," Jan replied.

"I was just thinking about taking a break and going for a swim. Do you feel like joining me? I have an extra suit you can wear."

"Oh, that sounds heavenly."

The two women changed, swam a few laps, and then relaxed in the hot tub.

"There's going to be a surprise at the party Saturday," Jan told Lizzie.

"Is someone going to jump out of a cake?" Lizzie asked.

Jan laughed. "Not out of a cake, but out of another room if that's okay."

"Sure it is. Who and when?"

"Drake told Ben and Carol that he couldn't get off work and wouldn't be here. Things changed, and he is able to be here after all. Would it be possible for him to hide in another room until everyone is seated?"

"He can wait in the office. I'll come get him right before dinner is served."

"That's perfect. He'll be here before the rest of us arrive. They are going to be so surprised. He hasn't been home since our wedding."

The cousins chatted a while longer before Jan went home. Lizzie pondered different ways of bringing Drake into the party. She had finally decided on a plan when she saw Dan coming toward the inn. *Should I tell Dan? Would he tell Megan? I don't want Megan to show up and ruin the Wagner's anniversary. He knows the party is for the Wagners.* Dan wouldn't be working that day, but he would be helping with the preparations. She decided it best not to mention Drake.

"Lizzie, you have a phone call," Ellen told her.

"Thanks, Mama."

She went to the office and picked up the phone, "This is Lizzie."

"Lizzie! They like the movie idea. I'd like to bring Webster Markham, the screen writer and Rachel Rockwood with me. She'll be playing your part, and wants to watch and learn."

"I hope this is Monty, or I'm hanging up."

"Of course it's me! Who else would have a crazy scheme like this on such short notice?"

"When would you like to come?"

"Do you have rooms available next week?"

"Yes, I do. How many will you need?"

"Two, one for Web and one for Rachel and me."

"How long will you need them?"

"At least a week or two, maybe longer."

"I'll book them for you for a week with an option for a second week. Will that work?"

"Perfect, thanks Lizzie."

"Thank you. I'm looking forward to seeing you."

"Great, I'll let you know when we arrive in Dallas."

"See you soon."

"Bye, Lizzie."

Lizzie hung up the phone smiling. *Granny will hate that Monty is bringing his girlfriend*, she thought.

Lizzie found Ellen sweeping the patio. She told her mom about the guests coming the next week. Ellen had forgotten to tell her that she had booked one of the rooms for that weekend. She found the name and gave it to her daughter. Lizzie went to the office and entered the information into the computer. Ann Wainrite would be staying for a week. Lizzie was pleased that three of the four rooms were booked.

Wade Adams opened the front door to the inn and said, "Anybody home?"

Lizzie came out of the office. "I'm sorry; I didn't hear you. Please, come in."

"Good morning," he said smiling at her. "I'm going to have a look around the site again. I thought you'd like to know that a reporter heard about the bodies. He's coming to do an interview at my office this afternoon. He may come out here snooping around. Call me if you see anyone that shouldn't be here."

"I will. How did a reporter find out?"

"I suspect one of the men talked about it, and the story circulated to the ear of a reporter or someone who knows a reporter," he said obviously annoyed.

"Thanks for letting me know. I'll tell the others."

"It looks like you're busy around here."

"For some reason, business picked up when word got around that Montgomery Powell had been here. The phone has been ringing nonstop. We're booking rooms and events with almost every phone call. The mess you see in here is part of the preparations for an anniversary party scheduled for Saturday."

"Imagine that," Wade said laughing. She liked his laugh and his smile.

"Monty will be here next week for a while with his girlfriend, Rachel Rockwood, and a screenwriter. People at Martin's wedding reception will probably get to meet them."

"Business will really start booming then," he said smiling at her. "I'll get down to the site and get out of your way before you put me to work," he teased. "I'll see you later."

"Bye, Wade."

So, Monty has a girlfriend. Wade grinned with satisfaction as he walked to his truck.

TWELVE

The discovery of the two bodies made the headlines of local newspapers and was the lead story for the local news casts. Soon the story spread to surrounding areas.

Travis Locke was relaxing and watching the evening news while he waited for a pizza to be delivered. "The skeletal remains of two individuals were found yesterday near Vernon," the anchorman reported. "More when we come back."

"Damn commercials," Locke said aloud as the doorbell rang. He hurried to pay the delivery boy and back to the living room. Something told him that he shouldn't miss that story.

When the commercials finally ended, Locke turned up the volume so that he wouldn't miss a thing. The anchorman reported, "Two bodies were found near the Paradise Creek Inn yesterday. Flood waters from the nearby creek unearthed part of the remains leading to the discovery. Officials have not yet identified the remains but say they appear to have been there for many years. The investigation is still in progress."

Locke sat deep in thought for a long time. He wondered if it could be possible. He went to his computer and found a map of the area. *It might be,* he thought. He decided to follow the story to see what other information would be found.

The final preparations for the Wagner's anniversary party were under way when James came out to the patio.

"Thunderstorms are predicted for this afternoon and evening. I'm going to get the cellar ready just in case," he told Lizzie.

"Thank you, Daddy. I sure hope it isn't like the last one," Lizzie replied.

"I hope it isn't either, but you'll have help here this time," he said grinning at her as he walked toward the cellar.

The decorating was complete and the food prepared when the waitresses arrived. They added a few finishing touches and then waited for the guests. The phone rang while Lizzie waited in the office for Drake.

"Paradise Creek Inn, how may I help you?" Lizzie answered.

"Is Montgomery Powell still staying there?"

"No, sir, he checked out?"

"Will he be coming back?"

"I'm not at liberty to disclose that information."

"That's all I needed to know," the man said and hung up.

Lizzie was staring at the phone thinking about the phone call when Drake tapped on the office door.

"Hi, Lizzie," he was smiling at her when she looked up.

"Hi, Drake, how are you?"

"Really well. How are you?"

"I'm good but busy, busy, busy these days. Would you like to wait here in the office or in one of the rooms for your entrance?"

"I'll wait in the office if that's all right. I can look out the window so I'll know when they get there."

"Do you have a vehicle we should hide?"

"They don't know I have a Harley, so they won't know it's mine."

"Your folks are going to be so excited that you came."

"What time are they supposed to be here?"

"In about thirty minutes."

"Mind if I stretch out on the sofa? It was a long ride."

"Be my guest. I need to do one last check on everything. You can wait and relax here. I'll come get you when it's time."

They smiled at each other as he settled on the sofa, and she closed the office door.

Storm clouds were building as family and friends of Ben and Carol Wagner were shown to the patio. Drake's parents were seated with their backs to the patio doors so that they would not be able to see him.

The table was large enough for six guests. Jan, Eli, Hart, and his wife Dawn were seated with Ben and Carol. Faith and her longtime boyfriend, Mike Foreman, were seated with Gage and his wife, Kirsten, at a table nearby. They were trying to inconspicuously save a seat for Drake.

James asked for everyone's attention, "Ladies and gentlemen, if you'll take your seats, dinner will be served shortly. I'd like to take this opportunity to welcome you to the inn. I'd also like point out that there appears to be a strong possibility of thunderstorms tonight. I'll keep an eye on the weather and keep you informed."

James nodded at Lizzie. She went to the office and said, "Drake, it's time."

They were both smiling in anticipation as they walked toward the patio. Eli saw Drake and tried to distract his parents. They were both listening to Eli when Drake walked outside. He moved behind them and covered their eyes with his hands, "Guess who!"

"Oh my word," Carol exclaimed at the same moment Ben said, "Drake? Is that you?"

Drake hugged both his parents and wiped a tear from his mother's cheek.

"What are you doing here? We thought you had to work."

"All part of my plan," he said smiling at them. "I was able to get off work after all."

"We're so glad you're here," Carol said through tears of joy.

After dinner, James started a video that had been created in honor of the happy couple. The photos that Jan had provided were included with photos others had supplied. Music began when the video ended. The anniversary couple had the first dance.

Ellen stepped out and whispered in her husband's ear. The two went inside. It was almost time to bring out the cake, and Lizzie wondered what was happening. James returned to the patio and stopped the music. "Ladies and gentlemen there is a severe thunderstorm a few miles over the county line that appears to be moving this way," he said. "If you will please follow Lizzie, the party will resume in the cellar."

A flash of lightning and the rumble of thunder added urgency to the request. The guests hurried down into the cellar and were pleased to find that everything had been prepared in anticipation of the storm. Dancing resumed when all of the guests were safely in the cellar. Ellen and Lois had placed the cake on the table as it started to rain.

Drake and Lizzie danced and talked. He was the only unaccompanied member of the Wagner family at the party. Thunder rumbled, lightening flashed, and the wind blew, but the guests were unconcerned. They were safe and enjoying the celebration.

When the thunder began to subside, James opened the cellar door. Thunder still rumbled in the distance but the rain had stopped. He went inside to listen to the local weather. When he was satisfied that the storms were over for the evening, he went back to the cellar.

"Ladies and gentlemen, the storm has passed. I believe it's safe to return to the patio."

Lizzie and Drake led the way out of the cellar. Drake had asked Lizzie to have dinner with him the next evening. She was about to answer when something caught her eye.

Megan was standing on the patio. She stood with fists at her sides, pure rage on her face. The moment she saw Drake she began to yell obscenities. She ranted and raved about how Drake had destroyed her life. Drake calmly told her that she was mistaken and reminded her of what she had done. She ran toward him and looked as if she were about to claw his face, but Dan intercepted her. He moved in front of her, picked her up, and carried her over his shoulder.

Megan kicked, screamed, and pummeled Dan's back as he made his way through the inn and out to his truck. Lizzie's heart broke for him when she saw the misery on his face. He must have heard Megan's tirade and Drake's response.

The party continued for another hour at Drake's insistence. "There's no reason to let a little temper tantrum ruin my parents anniversary," he said. "We still have cake, champagne, and music. The weather is nice, so Lizzie, if you will do me the honor." He took her hand and led her in a dance followed by his siblings, their partners, and gradually the other guests.

Drake was the last to leave that evening. "Lizzie, you never gave me your answer about dinner tomorrow night."

"I'd like that very much, Drake."

"I'll be here at seven." He smiled and kissed her cheek. Lizzie waved goodbye as he drove away on his Harley.

Lizzie had been waiting nervously when Drake arrived promptly at seven the following evening in his dad's truck. They drove into Vernon and had dinner at a local steak house. They talked and joked as they had in the past. Drake told her about Colorado, and she told him about the inn. He was particularly interested in her adventures with Montgomery Powell.

"Are you interested in him, Lizzie?"

"No, we're just friends. You know I don't date married men. Are you jealous after all this time?" Lizzie teased.

"No, no. I was curious that's all," Drake said looking uneasy.

Wade was sitting in a booth toward the back of the restaurant when Lizzie arrived with Drake. He waited until he was ready to leave to walk to their table.

"Hello, Lizzie," Wade said, eyeing Drake.

"Hi, Wade. This is my friend Drake Wagner. Drake this is Sheriff Wade Adams."

The two men shook hands and sized each other up.

"Nice to meet you, Sheriff."

"It's nice to meet you, too. I'm sorry to interrupt your dinner. If I could have a few moments with Lizzie, I won't have to drive out to the inn."

"Certainly, please join us," Lizzie said and noticed the irritation on Drake's face.

"Thank you. I won't take up much of your time," Wade said as he sat down. "I thought you'd like to know the latest news about the bodies that Dan found."

"Yes, I would," she replied. Drake's irritation was turning to interest.

"The information is going to be released to the press tomorrow. I thought you'd want to know in case reporters start showing up at your place."

"Do you think they will?"

"It's possible. I'll have my men out there to collect anything we left behind and fill in the hole. They can deal with any reporters that show up."

"What did you find out?"

"All indications are that the bodies have been buried for at least one hundred years. They were both male of the same height and build. They were probably hanged based on the damage to the cervical vertebrae."

"Wow," Drake said for lack of a better word.

Wade nodded. "We found a few coins that are most likely from the late 1800's and a tin cup. The pieces of leather we found could have been from a saddle or saddlebag."

"Do you have any idea who they were?" Lizzie asked.

"No, we probably never will. Any witnesses would have died long ago."

"My family will be relieved to hear this. Dan probably will too."

"Have you seen Dan today?"

"No, he had the weekend off. What's wrong?" Lizzie asked.

"He's had a rough weekend. I can't give you any details, but it might be a good idea for you and Mr. Wagner to go visit him. I'll leave you to your dinner. Have a good evening." Wade tipped his hat at Lizzie as he walked away and left the restaurant.

Drake and Lizzie continued their conversation while they finished their dinner. As they talked, Drake asked, "How long have Dan and Megan been married?" Lizzie told him everything she knew about the couple.

"Where does he live?" Lizzie gave Drake directions, and they were in Dan's driveway a short time later.

Dan looked as if he hadn't slept or eaten for weeks when he answered the door. He was glad they had come. He wanted to tell them what had happened.

One of Megan's friends had been the date of a Wagner family friend. When she saw Drake at the party, she had called Megan and left a message on the answering machine. Megan was gone when Dan got home from working cattle with his dad. He had no idea where Megan was but thought she was probably at her mom's. He went to the phone to call Roxanne and noticed there was a message on the answering machine. He felt sick when he heard it. He called Roxanne and found that Megan wasn't there.

He drove out to the inn hoping he wouldn't find her there but had been only a few minutes behind her. He reached the patio door as she started cursing Drake. Standing there not sure what to do, he listened as Drake calmly answered Megan's accusations revealing his side of the story.

He made the decision to take Megan home and sort things out there.

That was when he went outside and carried Megan to the truck. She had cursed, kicked, and hit him all the way back to town. Roxanne was waiting for them at the house. Megan burst into tears when she saw her mother and said that everyone had been so mean. She told her mother that Dan had hit her as she dialed the number to the sheriff's office. Dan felt the sheriff's presence might calm the situation and didn't try to stop her.

Roxanne knew Megan was lying. There were no marks on her. Dan had a number of bruises and scratches. When the sheriff arrived, the three of them decided to take Megan to the emergency room. They felt that she needed help and probably sedation. They waited outside while the doctor examined her. Dan needed to hear from Roxanne why Megan hated Drake and Lizzie so much. Roxanne told Dan the story, the same story that Lizzie and Drake had told.

According to Roxanne, Megan had seen a psychiatrist for months after she lost the baby and Drake left. The doctor said that Megan couldn't deal with the truth and had changed the story to cope. She had begun to believe the lie she told herself and others. Seeing Drake and Lizzie must have triggered something in her mind.

The doctor came out of the room and told them that Megan was calm. He thought that she needed psychological evaluation. He suggested that she be placed in the psychiatric ward in Wichita Falls for a while. Dan and Roxanne agreed and then went in to see Megan.

Dan had to know. He asked Megan if she loved him. When she said no, he asked why she had married him. She told him because she thought he would make lots of money on the rodeo circuit.

He had been an up and coming bull rider. His name becoming well known, and he was on his way to the national finals rodeo. He hadn't planned on getting hurt and never riding again. Since then, he had made his living working odd jobs until he was hired to work for the Fletchers.

Dan had been considering marriage counseling. They had had problems since his accident. When Megan saw Lizzie at the inn, she began accusing him of having an affair with her. He had explained a million times that he loved her. He liked Lizzie as a friend and boss, but that was all. He had told Megan repeatedly that he was not cheating on her. Now, he wondered why it mattered. She didn't love him and never had. It was obvious that marriage counseling wouldn't help.

Dan and Wade had taken Megan's things to Roxanne's house. Megan would live with her when she was released from the hospital. Dan would be filing for divorce and a restraining order on Monday. He suggested that Drake and Lizzie also file restraining orders. Megan would be getting out of the hospital soon.

Lizzie told Dan that he could take all the time he needed. His job would be waiting for him when he returned. Dan smiled and thanked her. He told her that he would be at work after he had finished his business. He needed to stay busy. Lizzie understood and didn't argue with him. Drake shook hands with Dan and told him how badly he felt about the situation. Dan assured him that it wasn't his fault. Megan had played them both.

Lizzie and Drake rode back to the inn in silence. They were both thinking about how one woman could destroy so many lives. Drake asked Lizzie if she would like to meet in town to file the restraining orders. She told him she would let him know after she talked to her family about it. He kissed her goodnight on the front steps and drove away. Lizzie went inside still feeling the warmth of the kiss on her lips. She fell asleep wondering why he would kiss her after all that had happened.

Early the next morning, Lizzie called her dad and told him that she had a lot to tell the family. When they arrived for breakfast, she shared the information Wade had given her and what had happened between Dan and Megan. They discussed the restraining order for some time.

Finally, Lois said, "I don't want that girl to show up and ruin another event. I know that the Wagners said that her little perfor- mance didn't matter, but it was uncomfortable for everyone. The party would have ended at that moment if Drake hadn't stepped in."

It was agreed that a restraining order should be filed. Lizzie called Drake, and they arranged to meet in town.

They had lunch at a local hamburger place they had frequented in the past. The burgers were as good as they had always been. They each ordered a milk shake to go before going to the courthouse.

Sheriff Adams was leaving the courthouse as Drake and Lizzie were going in.

"Hi, Wade. My folks said to thank you for keeping us up to date."

"It's my pleasure, Lizzie. Did you see Dan?"

"Yes, we did," Drake replied. "We're here to file restraining orders. Megan won't bother me, but I don't want her to bother my family."

"What makes you think she won't bother you? From what I've heard, you and Lizzie would be her main targets."

"I'll be going back to Colorado before she gets out of the hospital. I only had a few days off work."

"I hope you have a safe trip back," Wade said as he shook hands with Drake.

"Thanks, Sheriff."

"Bye, Wade"

"Let me know if you have any unwelcome visitors, Lizzie"

"I will."

Wade watched the pair go up the courthouse steps and couldn't help feeling relieved that Drake Wagner would be leaving soon.

Drake and Lizzie finished their business at the courthouse. Drake drove Lizzie back to her car and Lizzie asked, "When do you have to leave?"

"Tomorrow afternoon. I have to be back at work Wednesday morning."

"It's a shame you couldn't stay longer. Your family misses you."

"I know." He paused a moment, "Do you miss us, Lizzie?"

Lizzie was surprised. She didn't know what to say.

"You don't have to answer that. I thought we might have a chance if I should ever move back here."

"Are you moving back?"

"I might someday. I like my job and Colorado, but I'd come back if things were to change with my family. I'd come back for you."

"Aren't you rushing things a little bit?" Lizzie asked laughing.

"Probably, but I'd like for us to start over when you're ready."

"I see. How can we start over when we're so far apart?"

"When you're ready, we'll figure it out."

Drake walked Lizzie to her car and kissed her goodbye.

"Have a safe trip back to Colorado," she said as she drove away. She looked in her rearview mirror to see Drake standing there watching her go. She waved goodbye and drove on.

Dan was mowing the lawn in front of the inn when she returned. He stopped the mower and walked over to her. Lizzie told him the restraining orders had been filed. Dan told her that he had done the same. Megan would be served with the divorce papers when she arrived at her mother's house.

"I'm sorry about the other night, Lizzie. I didn't know Drake was going to be here or that she would behave that way. I would have kept a closer eye on her."

"It's my fault, Dan. I knew Drake would be here but decided not to tell you. I didn't want you to worry. I never dreamed she'd find out he was here."

"Well, I guess it was all for the best. I found out the truth. Now, I've got to put it behind me and move on with my life."

"It won't be easy, but you can do it. I have."

"Thanks, Lizzie," Dan said, and he restarted the mower.

THIRTEEN

The week went by quickly as the inn was cleaned and prepared for the weekend guests. Wade Adams had come with his men to do a final inspection of the dig site and to fill it in. The men went back to town, but Wade stayed for a little while visiting with the family over iced tea and coffee cake.

"Oh no," Wade said slapping his forehead. "I forgot to bring the reimbursement check."

"I'll be in town tomorrow. I could pick it up while I'm there," Lizzie offered.

"I should be at the office. If not, I'll leave it at the front desk."

"I'm not sure what time I'll be there. It's my day out with the girls tomorrow."

Wade laughed and then said, "I should be getting back. If you don't make it by the office, I'll mail it to you. Enjoy your day out with the girls," he teased.

"Bye, Wade," the family called in unison. He tipped his hat and winked at Lizzie before closing the door behind him.

Lizzie met Jan and Faith in town the following morning. The women went by the sheriff's office to pick up the check. Wade was out, but his deputy, Maddie Clifton, found the envelope with the check inside. She gave it to Lizzie, and girls day out began.

The three went to the spa, had lunch, and shopped. They decided to see a movie and then stopped for dinner and drinks before going home.

The inn was quiet when Lizzie returned. She turned the television set on in her room and settled in to watch the evening news before retiring for the night. She wasn't surprised to hear that Paradise Creek was on the nightly news again.

The anchor man reported the bones found near Vernon were believed to be more than one hundred years old and that the two men were probably hanged. The case would probably remain unsolved since it was likely that any witnesses were also deceased.

The report had again spread to surrounding areas. Travis Locke had watched with interest. He called information and asked for the number for the Paradise Creek Inn. He immediately dialed the number.

"Good evening, Paradise Creek Inn. How may I help you?"

"I'd like to book a room please."

"When would you like to have the room?" Lizzie asked

"Do you have a room available for the weekend?"

"Yes, we do. How long will you be staying?"

"Only the weekend, but if I decide to stay longer, will that be a problem?"

"No problem at all. When will you be arriving and how many are in your party?"

"I'll be arriving alone Friday evening."

"May I have your name, sir?"

"Travis Locke."

"We look forward to seeing you on Friday, Mr. Locke."

"Thank you, goodbye."

Lizzie worked throughout the week to make sure the guest rooms looked their best. It would be the first time that all four rooms were booked. She was excited and a little worried. Monty already loved the inn, and she hoped the other guests would be just as pleased. She had decided to put Monty's party next door to each other. Monty would have the same room he had during his previous stay on the east side of the house. Mr. Markham would be next door to Monty on the west side of the house. Mr. Locke would be across the hall from Monty. Ms. Wainrite would be across the hall from Mr. Markham. She wondered if it was Ms, Miss, or Mrs. Wainrite. She decided Ms. would do until she arrived.

On Thursday, finally satisfied with the rooms, Lizzie went downstairs to finish decorating for the wedding reception. It was earlier than she would have normally done the décor, but she would be preparing food for her guests and for Saturday's event. She wanted everything to go smoothly.

Lizzie finished and stood back to examine her work. She was pleased with the outcome and went to the kitchen to begin food preparation for the evening meal. Monty and his friends would be there for dinner.

"Lizzie, your friend Monty just called," Ellen told her. "They were leaving the Dallas airport and should be here within three hours."

"Thanks, Mama. We'll be ready. Should we tell Granny?" Lizzie asked grinning.

Ellen grinned too. "She'll be very unhappy with us if we don't. I'll call her."

Granny and James arrived an hour later. Granny had put her hair up and was wearing her best dress. James grinned at her and said, "Lizzie, I think your grandmother has a crush on your friend."

Lizzie hugged her grandmother. "Granny, are you wearing makeup?"

"What's wrong with a woman looking her best when meeting new people?" she asked annoyed.

"I have some bad news for you. Monty's girlfriend is coming, too."

"Why would that matter to me?" Granny replied in a huff.

James and Lois went into the dining area to relax and wait for their guests. Lizzie worked in the kitchen while Ellen answered the phone.

Montgomery Powell and his friends arrived shortly after seven. Introductions were made as Ellen checked them in. Lizzie showed them to their rooms and told them that a buffet was prepared for them when they were ready.

Webster Markham was the first to come downstairs. He was a short, stocky, middle aged man that appeared to be in good physical shape. The word pale came to mind when Lizzie first met him. He had white hair, light blue eyes, and a fair complexion. He seemed a bit surprised and uncomfortable to be the only one in the dining room.

"Please, help yourself to the buffet, Mr. Markham," Lizzie urged, handing him a plate.

"I prefer Web please. Am I the first to come down?" he asked looking ill at ease.

"Yes, but I'm sure the others will be along any moment."

Web reluctantly moved toward the buffet. He looked around the room awkwardly. He seemed to feel it necessary to say something. "This room is exactly as I pictured it from Monty's description. A fabulous scene should be written for this room. Is there WIFI access here?"

"Yes, but it may be slow if many people are using it."

"Is there someplace I can research if the WIFI isn't working?"

"I can set you up in the office if needed."

"Oh that would be wonderful, thank you," he said with obvious relief.

Monty came downstairs and joined them.

"Doing all right there, Web?"

Web nodded and sat down to his dinner.

"Web is kind of a recluse. He doesn't like crowds or places he isn't accustomed to. He'd much rather be alone in his apartment at his computer than around people. Maybe that's why he's so good at what he does."

Web looked up and smiled at Monty before focusing on his dinner.

"Did I happen to leave a red thumb drive behind the last time I was here?"

"Not that I'm aware of. Are you missing one?"

"Yeah, I thought I had it in my bag when I got on the plane. I probably just misplaced it. It's no big deal."

"I haven't seen anything like that, but I'll let you know if I do."

"That would be great, Lizzie. Thanks."

Monty turned as Rachel came down the stairs.

Rachel Rockwood was a beautiful woman with long wavy blonde hair and brown eyes that looked as if they never missed anything. She smiled and walked toward Monty. She stayed close to him while she took in her surroundings. She had made several movies and was a competent actress. Playing opposite Monty would be a big boost for her career.

After they had eaten their fill, Lizzie led them on a tour of the grounds. Monty and Web walked behind the two women discussing ideas for the movie they were to make. They discussed the inn as the setting of the movie and how it would be used to its best advantage. They debated about including the bodies that were found in the story.

"Monty has talked about nothing else but this inn and the movie since he got home," Rachel told Lizzie. "He fell in love with this place, and he absolutely adores you," she said.

Lizzie blushed. "We were pretty isolated while he was here. We became good friends."

Rachel seemed to be staring at Lizzie. Suddenly, Rachel asked,

"Is there a place where I can get my hair done?"

"When would you like to have it done?"

"As soon as possible."

"I'll call a friend of mine when we go back inside."

"That would be wonderful."

Lizzie called her hairdresser when the tour ended.

"Rachel, would eleven in the morning be too early?"

"That will be perfect. Thank you."

"You can ride into town with me. I need to pick up a few things, and I have plans for lunch. We'll need to leave at ten-thirty"

"Great. It's been a long day. I'm going upstairs now. Those two will probably talk for hours. Goodnight, Lizzie."

"Goodnight."

The two men talked a while longer, then said goodnight and went upstairs. Lizzie made a list of the things she would need the next day and retired for the night.

To Lizzie's surprise, Rachel came downstairs the next morning promptly at ten-thirty. She asked lots of questions on the way into town. Lizzie wasn't sure if she was curious or researching the role she was to play.

"How long has the inn been open?" Rachel asked

"A little over a year."

"I understand the house was renovated into the inn. How long did that take?"

"It took us nine months."

"How did the place look before you renovated?"

Lizzie described how the house looked and the renovations.

"So the grounds are almost the same as they were before. That's amazing. Has it been an exciting job?"

"Not at first, but business has been picking up since Monty crashed landed here."

"What do you think of Monty?"

"I've always been a fan. I have most of his movies in my

collection."

"No, I mean as a man. Do you think he's attractive?"

Lizzie looked at her for a moment puzzled before answering, "Yes, he's attractive."

"Would you go out with him if he asked?" Rachel asked making Lizzie feel a little like she was in high school.

"No, I don't date married men or men who are involved with someone else."

"Would you if he was single and available?"

"I'm not interested in dating anyone right now."

"You've been hurt haven't you? I can see it in your eyes. I'll bet you never let a man get too close. You probably prefer to be friends. Maybe a little harmless flirting, but otherwise men are kept at arm's length."

"Are you excited about the movie?" Lizzie asked trying to change the subject and wondering if Rachel was in the habit of saying whatever popped into her head.

"Oh yes. I'm very excited. I hope you don't mind, but I plan to study you so that I can bring authenticity to the part."

Rachel had already begun mimicking Lizzie's greeting to the guests. Lizzie found it a little unnerving but thought it was part of show business.

"Promise me you'll leave out any unflattering or bad habits," Lizzie joked.

"It's a deal. I can see why Monty is so taken with you. You're so real and easy to talk to."

Lizzie blushed and said, "Thanks," as she parked at the beauty salon.

Lizzie introduced Rachel to her hair dresser. Amanda was beside herself to have a celebrity in her shop. She assured Lizzie that Rachel would be in good hands and that she would call her when they were finished. Lizzie purchased the items she needed at the supermarket before meeting Faith for lunch.

Faith had been waiting only a few minutes when Lizzie entered the restaurant. Lizzie was about to sit down when Faith said, "I have something to tell you."

Faith looked so happy that Lizzie said, "You'd better tell me before you burst."

"Mike proposed last night," she said with tears of joy glistening in her eyes as she showed Lizzie her engagement ring.

"Oh that's fantastic! I'm so happy for you. Tell me every detail."

Faith obliged, and then she asked Lizzie if it would be possible to have the wedding and reception at the inn.

"Of course! Have you set the date?"

"We've decided on the last Saturday of April next year."

"I believe that day is open, but let me call to make sure." Lizzie's grandmother was manning the phone today while Ellen was available to attend to the guests.

"Granny, will you check to see if we have any events booked for the last Saturday in April of next year?" After a short pause, Lizzie said, "Good. We need to book that day for Faith's wedding. Thanks, Granny. I should be back in an hour or two. Okay, I'll tell her. Bye. It's all set. Granny said that she's thrilled for you."

The two women were talking about wedding plans when Lizzie's phone rang. It was time to collect Rachel and go back to the inn. Lizzie said goodbye to Faith and drove to Amanda's shop. Lizzie stopped in her tracks when she saw Rachel.

"Do you like it, Lizzie?" Rachel asked.

"Um, yeah. It looks nice." Lizzie replied. She was telling the truth, but it was such a surprise that Lizzie didn't know what to say. Rachel's hair was cut and colored to look exactly like hers.

Lizzie had recovered by the time she and Rachel returned to the inn. Rachel went in search of Monty, while Lizzie began preparing for the arrival of her other two guests.

Travis Locke was the first to arrive. He was a tall lean man with thinning gray hair. Lizzie judged him to be near her dad's age. His gray eyes peered through a pair of wire rimmed glasses. He was dressed in jeans and a lightweight long sleeved cotton shirt. He was employed at a university in Lubbock. He looked so much the scholarly type that Lizzie mentally nicknamed him the professor.

Lizzie showed him to his room and had returned to the lobby when her final guest arrived. Ann Wainrite was tall and slender with kind brown eyes and a lovely smile. Her silver hair fell across her forehead in soft bangs. She was dressed in what appeared to be an expensive tailored suit.

That evening at dinner, Lizzie informed her guests that a wedding reception would be taking place the following evening. The host of the party would be honored to have them join in the festivities if they would like. Her guests were pleased with the invitation and said they would be happy to attend.

"Monty, do you remember Martin Thomas?" Lizzie asked.

"The chopper pilot?"

Lizzie nodded. "He's the groom."

During dinner, the guests visited and got acquainted with one another. The professor asked Lizzie about the recent discovery of the bodies.

"I heard on the news about the two bodies that were found here. How did you happen to find them?"

"Our hired hand made the discovery when repairing fence near the creek."

"Have the authorities finished the exhumation?"

"Yes, they have."

"Did they leave the grave open?"

"No, they've filled it back in."

"What sorts of things did they find?"

Lizzie was becoming more wary as the questioning progressed. She wasn't sure how much she should divulge. "As far as I know, only what has been mentioned on the news. Maybe the sheriff would be the best person to talk to. We weren't actually watching them dig."

"I'm sorry about asking so many questions, but I find this all fascinating. I work in the archeology department at the university."

"That's quite all right. We have quite a few questions ourselves. The sheriff said he would tell us when he finds out anything."

"Oh yes, I understand completely."

Mr. Locke excused himself to visit with the other guests and finished his dinner.

After dinner, the professor asked if it would be acceptable to walk the grounds and smoke his pipe. Lizzie assured him that it was. He thanked her and went outside. Rachel decided to go out to the pond while Monty and Web discussed the screenplay. Ms. Wainrite relaxed by the pool.

Rachel had thought about fishing but chose to try one of the paddle boats instead. Fishing wasn't really her idea of relaxation. She paddled to the center of the pond and sat quietly taking in the view. She could see practically everyone from here. She could see Ms. Wainrite sitting on the patio by the pool. She seemed be staring into the kitchen. Rachel followed her gaze. Lizzie and her family were inside clearing away dinner.

She glanced toward the bedroom windows and noticed that the light was on in Mr. Locke's room. She looked toward her room just as the light went on. *Monty must be up there with Web. Those two are obsessed with this movie*, she thought. She was a little put out. Monty hadn't been paying much attention to her. All he could talk about was the movie, or Lizzie. Movement to her left caught her attention. Someone was opening the cellar door, but the Fletchers were all inside. *Maybe it was Web*, she thought, *but why would he be in the cellar*.

She turned slightly to her right, and she could see Mr. Locke walking along the creek. He had gone beyond the grounds of the inn. He would take a few long steps, stop, and look around before taking a few more all the while puffing furiously at his pipe.

She decided to try and drag Monty away from the screenplay and started back to the house. As she approached Ms. Wainrite, she noticed that a book was in her lap. "It's a lovely evening isn't it," she said trying to make polite conversation.

"Yes, it is."

"What are you reading?"

"*Death on the Nile*, it's one of the books from the inn collection."

"What's it about?"

"A murder takes place on a cruise down the Nile River. The very clever detective Hercule Poirot is onboard to solve the case."

"That sounds interesting. Let me know when you've finished. I'll read it, and we can discuss it. Sort of like a book club."

Ann Wainrite hesitated, "Certainly."

"I'm going see if I can tear Monty away from Web. It's too nice an evening to waste it inside."

Rachel walked inside toward the stairs and saw Web coming out of Lizzie's office. "How long have you been in there?"

"Oh not long, half an hour maybe," he answered startled.

"Have you been near the cellar?"

"No, I've been inside all evening. Why?"

"I saw someone by the cellar and thought it was you. I thought you and Monty were working on the script."

"I haven't seen Monty since dinner."

"That's odd," Rachel said sounding confused.

"What's odd?"

"It's probably nothing, just my imagination."

Web looked at her and hurriedly said, "Goodnight."

"Goodnight," she said and pondered what she had seen as she made her way upstairs. *Who was the man by the cellar? I'm almost certain it was a man. And why was Ms. Wainrite's book upside down. Why was Mr. Locke walking like that and why was he outside the grounds?* She tried the door to her room. It was locked. *Why would Monty have the door locked if he's inside?* She took out her key and opened the door. The light was still on when she went inside, but there was no sign of Monty. *Maybe he's on the balcony*, she thought. She walked out onto the balcony, looked down, and saw Monty was crossing the patio toward the inn. *If Monty was out there and Web was in the office, who was in our room?*

Ann Wainrite watched Rachel go inside and Lizzie's family say their goodnights. She stood, went inside, and sat down to watch Lizzie preparing for the next day. After a few moments, she asked, "May I help? I'm restless this evening and could use something to occupy my hands."

"Certainly. I'm preparing and chopping these vegetables for tomorrow." Lizzie took out another knife and cutting board for Ann to use.

"I've never been in such an isolated place before. How do you stand it?"

Lizzie laughingly replied, "I grew up here. This was my grandmother's house before we converted it."

"I don't mean to be insulting," Ann said apologetically. "I'm used to the city where everything is within a moments reach. How far is it to nearest city?"

"No apology needed. The nearest big city would be Dallas. It's about three hours away from here. The nearest town is only half an hour away."

"Have you lived here your entire life?"

"I lived in a big city for a while. I eventually became accustomed to it, but it never felt like home."

"Which city did you live in?"

"I lived in Chicago and worked in a hotel there. I always dreamed of owning a place like this. I jumped at the chance when it was offered. What brings you to our inn?"

"I live on the east coast. A friend of mine thought I needed to get away for a while. She said time and distance is the best cure for a broken heart. She had one of your business cards and here I am," she said as she smiled.

"I'm sorry you've been hurt. I know it doesn't feel like it now, but you'll survive," Lizzie assured her.

"Sounds like the words of a woman with experience. Do you mind telling me about it?"

Lizzie hesitated a moment before deciding that sharing might benefit them both. "I've survived heart break twice actually. One longtime boyfriend informed me that another woman might be carrying his baby. Then a few years later, I discovered that my new fiancé already had a wife. Now, I'm here running this inn."

"I'm so sorry you had to go through that. How long has it been since this happened?"

"The first was about seven years ago and the second two years ago."

"Do you ever consider trying again? You know what they say about the third time being the charm."

Lizzie laughed. "I'm so busy with the inn that I don't have time to think about it. Would you like to talk about your experience?"

Ann smiled sadly. "I'm not quite ready to talk about it. I hope you understand. Thank you for sharing your story. It does give me hope that the pain will go away."

"You're quite welcome. I understand completely. Let me know if there is anything I can do."

Ann smiled and said, "Goodnight Miss Fletcher."

"Goodnight, Ms. Wainrite."

Lizzie made preparations for the next day's event until late in the evening. She retired only after her guests had gone upstairs for the night.

Saturday was filled with attending to her guests and preparing for the reception. Lizzie was thankful that her family had come to help. When the waitresses that she had hired arrived, Lizzie put them to work on the final details.

The reception was a huge success. The newlyweds and their guests were thrilled to meet the celebrities. Monty and Rachel were extremely gracious about posing for pictures and signing autographs. Ms. Wainrite and Mr. Locke said goodnight early. Web had chosen to stay in his room to work on the movie script.

Monty and Rachel went upstairs at midnight when the last members of the wedding party had gone. Lizzie worked for half an hour taking down the party decorations and cleaning the kitchen. She decided that cleaning the patio could wait until daylight and went to bed.

Lizzie was preparing breakfast for her guests the next morning when Ellen and Lois arrived.

"Where's Daddy?" she asked.

"He's going to clean up the patio before coming in," Ellen told her.

James quietly opened the kitchen door. His face was gray, and he seemed to be ill.

"Mom, Ellen please close the blinds and keep our guests inside. Lizzie, see if you can get in touch with Wade Adams. I need to go back outside."

"James, what's wrong?" Ellen asked.

"There's a dead man in our pool," he said then went back to the patio.

The three women stared after him in disbelief. They looked at each other for a moment and then hurried to their assigned tasks.

Lizzie walked outside and stood beside her dad. "Wade is on his way," she told him.

"Thank goodness. I hope he gets here soon."

Lizzie stared at the dead man. He was wearing a black t-shirt with long sleeves, black pants, and black boots. He was lying draped over one end of the waterfall with his head and shoulders in the water. The water near his head was slightly red. Lizzie and James stood guard over the man's body while they waited for the sheriff.

FOURTEEN

Wade Adams frowned as he hung up the phone. *Another body at the inn! What's happening out there?* He wanted an excuse to see Lizzie again, but this wasn't what he had in mind. Plans for asking Lizzie to dinner would have to wait. If it was murder, he would have to view everyone at the inn as a possible suspect, including Lizzie and her family. He shook his head and tried to dismiss the thought. He hoped it was an accident and it would all be over soon.

The sheriff, his investigative team, and Dr. Hughes arrived at the inn to find a nervous and concerned Fletcher family. Ellen and Lois were waiting for them in the foyer and led the way to the patio where James and Lizzie stood guard over the man in the pool.

"Have you moved or touched anything?" Wade asked.

"I checked for a pulse but tried not to disturb anything," James replied.

"This is my deputy Craig Dodson. He has some routine questions for you. I'd appreciate it if you would all go inside with him while we work out here."

Deputy Craig Dodson led the stunned family back into the

house. They all seemed to be lost in their own thoughts as they sat down.

"Who found the body?" he asked.

"I did," James answered.

"Can you describe what happened?"

"We came early this morning to help with the cleanup. I walked around the house to the patio instead of coming inside. I saw something big and black beside the pool. I decided to start cleaning there. As I got closer, I realized it was a man. I called out to him, but there was no response. I checked for a pulse but didn't find one. I came inside and asked my mom and wife to keep our guests inside. I asked Lizzie to contact the sheriff. I went back outside to make sure nothing was disturbed." James sat back breathless when he had finished.

"What time did you arrive this morning?" the deputy asked.

"It was probably around seven-thirty."

"Who arrived with you?"

"My wife, Ellen, and my mother, Lois," James answered.

"About what time did you discover the body?"

"It couldn't have been much later than seven thirty-five".

"Did you touch or move anything other than checking for a pulse?"

"I picked up some scraps of paper as I came around the house. I dropped them in the trash can before I saw him. I didn't touch anything else."

"What time did you call the sheriff's office Miss Fletcher?"

"Immediately, after Daddy asked me to. I'm not sure of the time. It didn't occur to me to look."

"What did you do then?"

"I went outside to tell Daddy that you were on your way. I stayed with him until you arrived."

"Mrs. Fletcher?"

"Yes," Ellen and Lois answered in unison.

"Mrs. Ellen Fletcher, what did you do upon arriving this morning?"

"I came to the kitchen to help Lizzie with breakfast and any cleanup that needed to be done."

"What did you do after the body was discovered?"

"I closed the blinds so that our guests wouldn't see the body if they came down and tried to stay busy with breakfast and cleaning until you arrived."

"Mrs. Lois Fletcher, what did you do?"

"I helped Ellen and kept an eye out for the guests. Why are you asking us all these questions?"

"I'm trying to get an idea of everyone's activities and to corroborate times. I know this isn't pleasant but finding a body never is."

The Fletcher family couldn't argue with that.

"Miss Fletcher, how many guests are staying here at the moment?"

"We have five guests."

"What are their names and which rooms are they in? Would it be possible to get their phone numbers and addresses from you?"

Lizzie went to the office, printed a copy of the information, and gave it to the deputy. She wasn't comfortable with all the questions. The deputy seemed to be a particularly suspicious man. His questions were abrupt, and his manner bordered on rude.

"There was a wedding reception here last night?" the deputy asked.

Lizzie nodded.

Lizzie answered his questions about who the guests were, what time they left, and details of the evening as best she could. She couldn't remember every detail. She had been very busy.

"Excuse me," she interrupted the deputy. "Are we suspects?" she asked.

"At this point we have to consider everyone a possible suspect at least until we have more information."

"Do we need an attorney?" James asked.

"That is your right, Mr. Fletcher, if you wish. This is a preliminary investigation. We're trying to piece together as much information as possible to figure out what happened here. What time do you expect your guests to come down?"

"They should be coming down for breakfast any minute," Lizzie answered. "I need to get the food prepared."

"I don't have any more questions for you at the moment. Please, wait for Sheriff Adams to inform your guests about the man in the pool. If you'll excuse me, I'll go and see if the team has any news," he said as he walked out onto the patio and closed the door.

Ellen walked over to James, and they held each other close. "Did I understand him to say that anyone who has been here since last night could be a suspect? I don't like this at all," Ellen said.

"I don't either. Until they know more, what can we do?" James replied.

"James, do you think...?

"I don't know, Ellen."

Granny was setting the tables for breakfast. She looked worried. "Hmmm, I wonder," Granny said under her breath.

Lizzie prepared breakfast and wondered about the man. *Who was he? Could he have been connected to Rob?*

Once outside, Deputy Dodson reported the information he had gotten from the Fletchers to the sheriff. "They seemed to be in total shock. They were beginning to come around toward the end of the questioning. Miss Fletcher asked if they were suspects, and Mr. Fletcher asked if they needed an attorney. I gave them the standard answers."

Sheriff Adams stared at him for a moment. He didn't want to think of the Fletchers as suspects. He had grown fond of all of them and Lizzie in particular. He had to put his feelings aside for now. He knew it was good to have them questioned by an objective third party. Unfortunately, his senior deputy still needed to work on his people skills. "Thanks, Craig. I'll go and talk with them now."

Wade went inside to find the Fletcher family trying to stay busy. They looked up from their work as he walked into the room. They all had worry and fear on their faces.

"I'm so sorry about all the questions. All of the information that we can gather will help us to figure out who that man is and why he was killed."

"It's all been pretty scary," Ellen answered.

"I know. I wish it didn't have to be, but a man has been murdered here. It's a scary business. We need to find the responsible party as soon as we can."

"So it was murder?" Lizzie asked.

"Yes. Unfortunately, the killer may still be here."

The Fletcher family stared at him, speechless, and obviously frightened.

After a moment James asked, "What have you found so far?"

"We don't know a lot more than you do at the moment. The man had no identification on him. The way he was dressed indicates that he didn't want to be seen. There was a digital camera at the bottom of the pool. It appears to be an expensive one. It may have been his, or it may belong to one of your guests. If the camera was his, he could have been a reporter or paparazzi. The bodies found here would be interesting to reporters, and your guests would be interesting to either group."

Wade let them take in the information before continuing, "I believe you've given Dodson a list of everyone who was here last night with arrival and departure times."

"I'm not absolutely certain about times. It was pretty busy around here," Lizzie answered.

"I understand. We'll be talking with everyone on the list. We'll also need to interview your guests."

"They should be down shortly for breakfast."

"What vehicles outside belong to you or your guests?"

"Monty, Rachel, and Web came in a rental. I believe it's a silver Cadillac. Mr. Locke drove the blue Chevy pickup. Ms. Wainrite arrived in a cab. Mom, Dad, and Granny were in the red Dodge Durango. I have the green Jeep Wrangler. Is that important?"

"We don't know yet. Please, don't tell them what's been going on. We can learn a lot from their initial reactions. Do you have a room available that we can use as a command post?"

"You can use my office," Lizzie answered.

"That should do nicely. Thank you," Wade said.

There was a tap on the door, and the deputy opened it slightly, "Sheriff, the body is ready to be moved."

"I'm needed outside. I'll talk with y'all again as soon as I can."

The investigative team met near the fishing pond in hopes that no one at the inn would overhear their conversation. "What do you know so far Doc?" Wade asked Dr. Hughes.

"It looks like he was hit on the head from behind with a heavy jagged object. I don't see any sign of struggle. He was probably lying in that position when he was attacked. It's possible that he was trying to retrieve the camera. He may have known his attacker or was taken by surprise. He's probably been dead approximately four to six hours. I'll be more accurate after I've examined him in my lab. I'll ride back to town with the body and get started unless you need me to stay."

"Thanks Doc. I don't know of any reason you need to stay."

Dr. Hughes was a short stout man with a full head of brown hair. No one was sure of his age, and he never volunteered it. He was one of six doctors in the city of Vernon. He was chosen to serve as county medical examiner primarily because he had the convenience of a large basement beneath his office. The doctor waved goodbye as he opened the door to the medical examiner's van.

"Dodson, what have you got?" Wade asked.

"We've taken his fingerprints and photographed him. We'll start the identification process when we get back to town. We'll use dental records if necessary. Every vehicle on the property has been accounted for. This was found in one of the flower beds."

The deputy handed the plastic evidence bag to Wade. Inside was a large rock with a jagged edge.

"That looks like blood and hair to me."

"Yes, sir. We've taken a sample. We'll have it analyzed to see if it matches the victim."

"There was no media card in the camera. Nothing found on the body either," Lodge said.

"Did you find a media card when searching the grounds?"

"No, sir."

"Anything else?"

"I found this," one of the team members said. "It may not have anything to do with the case."

The sheriff took the bag and examined it. Inside was a piece of note paper. On the paper was written: *Meet me poolside at two.*

"Maybe, maybe not. Good work Reed. We'll keep it to ourselves for now. I want fingerprints from everyone at the inn. I also want a handwriting sample. Do we have a decent photo of the victims face?"

"Yes, sir."

"If there's a printer in the office here, make several copies."

Wade continued as the team photographer went about his task. "We'll be using the inn office as a command post. You can contact me there when you find something."

The photographer returned with the photos.

"I want everyone who has been here in the past twelve hours to have a look at the man's face. Baker, take the samples to the lab for analysis. Then take Maddie with you and talk to everyone on last night's guest list. Make sure that you show them that picture."

"Yes, sir."

"The victim wasn't dressed for warm weather. He was dressed to hide in the shadows. All of the vehicles here have been accounted for. His shoes aren't worn down. I doubt he walked thirty miles from town to get here especially dressed like that. Dodson and Lodge, you're with me. The rest of you, see if you can find a vehicle that is someplace it doesn't belong."

The team scattered to their assigned tasks as the sheriff and his deputies walked toward the inn. "It's time to talk with the guests, boys."

Sheriff Adams was happy to see that all of the guests had come down stairs and were enjoying their breakfast. They seemed oblivious to the presence of his team. He had given Dodson and Lodge instructions to search the guest rooms while he kept everyone busy downstairs. They were to collect anything that looked pertinent to the case. Especially a media card for the waterlogged digital camera.

The guests looked up in surprise when the three men entered the room.

"Ladies and gentlemen, I'm Sheriff Wade Adams of Wilbarger County. These men are my deputies Dodson and Lodge. We're here to investigate a crime that took place on the grounds of this inn sometime between midnight and seven-thirty this morning."

"What happened, Sheriff?" Monty asked.

"Mr. Fletcher found a man in the swimming pool when he arrived this morning. We are investigating that man's murder."

The guests sat silent for a moment and then all were asking questions at once.

"Lizzie, did you know about this?"

"Why didn't you tell us?"

"Are we in danger?"

"Who was he?"

Only Mr. Locke made no comment. He seemed to be speechless.

"I asked the Fletcher family not to tell anyone until we had more information."

"Sheriff, I demand to know what is going on," Ms. Wainrite said sternly.

"In due time, ma'am," he told her. "I am going to have to ask each of you for your fingerprints and your signature."

Gasps were heard around the room.

Wade held up his hand to quiet them and said, "This is only a routine procedure so that we can eliminate your fingerprints from those found at the scene. It will save valuable time if we have your signatures beside your prints."

Everyone reluctantly murmured their consent. Dodson and Lodge slipped upstairs to search while the sheriff fingerprinted the people in the dining room.

"Lizzie, let's start with you."

It took some time to take fingerprints from the Fletchers and their five guests. When they had finished, the sheriff told them that he would like to interview each of them privately in Lizzie's office. Dodson and Lodge came down stairs unobserved. They stood at the back of the room out of sight.

"I'm going to meet with my deputies for a moment. You will be called one by one to the office. Try to remember every detail of last evening."

The three men went into the office and closed the door.

"Did you find anything?" Wade asked.

"We found a locked box in Locke's room but no key. There was nothing of interest in Wainrite's room," Dodson answered.

"Laptops and flash drives in Markham's room. There was nothing pertinent in the room shared by Powell and Rockwood," Lodge replied as he placed Markham's items on a table.

"I'd like for Lodge to stay with the Fletchers and their guests. Don't let anyone go back to the rooms."

Sheriff Adams radio squawked. "Sheriff, do you read me?"

"What've you got?"

"We found the car. It was hidden across the creek in a shelterbelt about a mile away. Looks like the guy had been practically living in it. He was a P. I."

"A Private Investigator?"

"Yes, sir. We found a laptop, his identification, and his car keys inside the car."

"Bring anything we might need to look at to the inn. Have the car towed into town for processing."

"Yes, sir."

Wade went back into the dining room. "Ladies and gentlemen, it's going to be a little longer before we can start the interview process. More evidence has been discovered that needs my attention. In the meantime, please remain in here. We are currently searching the inn and the grounds for evidence. Thank you for your cooperation."

The guests were all open mouthed in astonishment.

The men arrived with the evidence from the car. One man stood guard outside the office door while the others went inside with the sheriff.

"It was an old brown Chevy Impala. The car couldn't be seen from here or anywhere on the grounds. He had it parked so that it was difficult to see from any direction," the deputy said. "We would have missed it if the sun hadn't been shining on the chrome bumper. The registration checks out with the name on the license in his wallet."

"Sam Hawk, Private Investigator. It looks like the same man. His driver's license shows him to be from Dallas. He didn't carry much cash and only one credit card. Maybe this computer will tell us who he was investigating."

Wade opened the laptop. Photos taken of the inn popped up when the sheriff touched the keys. "Some of these were taken before these guests arrived. Look at this, photos of the dig site where those two bodies were found. Lizzie and Dan seem to be the focus of several of them. These photos are of each of the Fletchers alone at different times. Here are photos of the current guests when they arrived. There doesn't seem to be any from yesterday."

"What do make of it, Sheriff?"

"I don't know. It seems for every answer we find we end up with twice as many questions. Dodson, get hold of Dan Hayes and have him come into the office for an interview. He might know something since he's in the photos. Find out if Megan Hayes is competent for an interview. If she is, arrange for her to come into the office. Reed, put the evidence you found on the table here behind the desk with the rest. I may use it in the interview process. See if you can find out who hired this guy and who he was investigating."

The deputies went about their assigned tasks while Sheriff Adams sat deep in thought. *Does someone have a grudge against one of the Fletchers or maybe all of them?* He sighed as he stood and called Lizzie in for the interview.

"Lizzie, if you don't mind, we'll start with you again."

Lizzie followed Wade to her office. She was shaking as she sat down in the chair usually reserved for guests. "I'm not used to sitting on this side of the desk," she joked.

"I know, Lizzie. I'm sorry to start with you, but I have a reason. I'd prefer your guests didn't know all the facts yet."

"Do you have new information?"

"We found a few items in the guest rooms that probably mean nothing. My deputies found the man's car across the creek. We'll keep searching the area in and around the inn to make sure we don't miss anything that might be important."

"Let me know if I can help in any way."

"The best help I can ask for right now is to keep your guests calm."

"I'll try," Lizzie answered doubtfully.

"Dodson has already asked you most of the questions. I have a few more since we have some new evidence. Do you recognize this man?" he asked showing her the picture of the victim.

"No. Is this the man in the pool?"

"Yes, does the name Sam Hawk mean anything to you?"

"No."

"No one you went to school with or met somewhere in the past by that name?"

"Not that I can remember."

"We believe the victim is Sam Hawk, a private investigator," Wade looked at her closely.

Lizzie was surprised. "A private investigator? Here? Why?"

"That's what we're trying to find out. Is there any reason why someone would investigate you or your family?"

Lizzie hesitated for a second, "Not that I'm aware of."

"This laptop was found in the man's car. Look at these photos. What's the first thing that comes to your mind?"

Lizzie looked at the photos on the laptop. She was silent while she scrolled through them. She was cold and trembling when she finished.

"Dodson, get Miss Fletcher some water please."

"Yes, sir," Dodson answered startling Lizzie. She was unaware that he had been in the room.

"Does anything come to mind? Any reason someone would be investigating you or your family?"

"The pictures of Dan and I suggest it could be Megan," Lizzie answered. "If she really believes that Dan and I were having an affair, she might have hired him."

"Anyone else?"

Lizzie hesitated again before answering, "No."

"Can you identify any of the items on the table?"

"The rock looks like it came from the flowerbed near the pool. The note paper looks like the notepads we have available here. I don't recognize anything else."

"Do you know which room the notepad was in?"

"I order them in bulk. There are pads like these all over the inn."

"Thank you, Lizzie. Please keep all of this to yourself until I've interviewed everyone."

Lizzie left the room.

"Dodson, have one of the men collect all of those pads and see if the note may have been torn from one of them. We'll wait to discuss the interviews until we've finished. Let's have James Fletcher in now."

The sheriff interviewed each of the Fletchers in turn asking them the same questions he had asked Lizzie. He watched their reactions hoping for a clue to any reason they would be under surveillance. Each had hesitated when he asked if they were aware of anyone who would investigate them. They recognized the same items that Lizzie had recognized.

FIFTEEN

While her family was being interviewed, the guests began to get restless. Lizzie did her best to keep them calm. She kept food and beverages available and movies playing on the big screen TV.

"I don't understand why we can't go up to our rooms," Ms. Wainrite said.

"Because they're searching our rooms," Mr. Locke answered.

"Why would they search our rooms?"

"They're searching the entire inn and its grounds," Lizzie replied.

"They think one of us could be the killer," Rachel giggled. She seemed to find the situation entertaining.

"Do you know the man that was killed, Lizzie?" Monty asked.

"No. I keep wondering why he was here and how he ended up in our pool."

"Ms. Wainrite, the sheriff would like to see you now," Ellen said as she returned to the room. Ann Wainrite stood and walked toward the office. She sat down across from the sheriff and waited.

"I'm going to ask you some routine questions Ms. Wainrite. I have asked everyone who has been interviewed the same questions. We're trying to find out who the man was and why he was killed."

"I understand, Sheriff."

"Will you verify your name, address, and telephone number please?"

Ms. Wainrite complied.

"How did you hear about this inn on the east coast?"

"A friend of mine had some of the inn's business cards. I needed to get away, so I decided to visit Texas."

"When did you arrive at the inn?"

"It was about eight o'clock Friday night."

"Did you drive?"

"I arranged to fly to the local airport and was brought here by cab."

"I understand that you and the other guests attended the wedding reception that was held here last night. Did you stay for the entire party?"

"There was too much love and happiness for my taste. I went to my room at ten-thirty."

"What did you do then?"

"I got ready for bed and read a book until it was quiet enough to fall asleep."

"Did you see or hear anything after the party guests left?"

"No."

"Do you recognize this man?" Wade showed her the photo of the victim.

She glanced at the photo and said, "No."

"Does the name Sam Hawk mean anything to you?"

"No."

"Do you recognize any of the items on the table behind me?"

"That camera is similar to one that I have."

"Did you bring your camera with you?"

"No. I didn't plan on taking any pictures."

"I'd like for you to look at these photos." The sheriff turned the laptop so that she could see.

She scrolled through the snapshots on the laptop and said, "Where did you get this?"

"We believe this laptop belonged to the victim. It was found in his car."

"Why would he have photos of me?"

"He was a private investigator. We were hoping you could tell us."

"I have no idea, Sheriff."

"Thank you, Ms. Wainrite. If anything comes to mind that you think might have something to do with this case, please, let us know. I'd appreciate it if you would keep the details of this interview to yourself until we have interviewed everyone. You may return to the dining room now."

"I'd call her an ice queen," Dodson said as she closed the office door.

"You're right. She had no reaction at all until she saw those photos. Something unnerved her about one of them. Did you notice which one?"

"She didn't appear to linger over any of them."

"Who's left to interview?"

"We haven't interviewed Montgomery Powell, Webster Markham, Travis Locke, or Rachel Rockwood."

"Send in Montgomery Powell. I hope he doesn't decide this calls for an academy award performance."

Dodson smiled and left the room. A short time later, Monty sat in the chair opposite the sheriff.

"It's good to see you again, Sheriff. I only wish it was under better circumstances."

"You look much more like the man on the movie screen than you did the first time I saw you."

Monty laughed. "I believe I've made a full recovery."

"I understand you're here doing some writing."

"I thought my crash here and this inn would make a great movie."

"When did you arrive?"

"We drove in Thursday evening around seven o'clock."

"We?"

"Web and Rachel traveled with me."

"I see. Did you drive all the way from California?"

"We flew into Dallas, rented a car, and drove out here."

"What time did you leave the party last night?"

"Rachel and I stayed until everyone had gone."

"What time would you say that was?"

"Midnight or close to it."

"What did you do then?"

"We went to bed and well... you know," Monty said and winked.

The sheriff cleared his throat. "Did you hear or see anything after you went upstairs that might be important to this case?"

"I was sound asleep the rest of the night."

"Do you recognize this man?" he asked sliding the photo to Monty.

"Hmm, I don't think so. There is something familiar about him though."

"Have you seen him here?"

"No. He looks like someone I know in California."

"Do you recognize the name Sam Hawk?"

"Sam Hawk, Sam Hawk. No I don't. It would be a cool name for an actor or a character in a movie."

"I guess it would. Do you recognize any of the items on the table behind me?"

"That looks like Web's laptop and gear. I don't recognize anything else."

"I'd like you to look at the photos on this laptop."

Monty scrolled through the photos. "Was he paparazzi or a reporter? These pictures cover a lot of time."

"He was a private investigator."

Monty looked up in surprise. For the first time he seemed to take the interview seriously. "Who was he investigating?"

"We don't know yet. Could he have been investigating you?"

Monty paused for a moment before answering, "My divorce isn't final. Maybe my soon to be ex-wife is trying to find something that she can use against me."

"Thank you, Monty. Keep the interview details to yourself for now, and let us know if you think of anything that might help in this investigation."

"Sure thing, Sheriff," and with that Monty left the room quickly.

Dodson grinned and said, "Not a bad performance."

"The words private investigator got his attention. I'd be willing to bet that he thinks someone other than his wife hired the investigator."

"He was sure in a hurry to get out of here."

"Let's see what Webster Markham can tell us."

Sheriff Adams looked across the desk at the man standing there. *How can anyone be healthy and be that pale?* he thought.

"Mr. Markham I understand you arrived at the inn with Mr. Powell and Miss Rockwood."

"Yes, yes I did."

"Do you recall what time that was?"

"Shortly after seven o'clock Thursday evening."

"What time did you leave the wedding reception last night?"

"I didn't go to the reception. I don't care for crowds, particularly when I don't know anyone. I decided to stay in my room and work on my script.

"I see. Did you come down for any reason during the night?"

"N...no, I fell asleep while writing. I woke up some time later and got into bed"

"Did you see or hear anything that might be important to this case?"

"No."

Wade slid the photo of the dead man toward Web, "Do you recognize this man?"

Web cringed and said, "No, I don't."

"Does the name Sam Hawk mean anything to you?"

Web paused for a moment before saying, "No."

"Do any of the items on the table behind me look familiar?"

"Why do you have my laptop and flash drives?"

"We've collected anything that might give us some answers. Does it appear that there is anything missing or anything there that isn't yours?"

Web looked more closely then said, "Everything there is mine. I don't see anything missing. I object to my personal property being taken from my room."

"It will be returned unharmed as soon as we have finished with it. I'd like for you to look at the photos on this laptop."

Webster scrolled through the photos, "Why have you invaded my privacy? I demand to know why you have photos of me."

"We didn't take these photos, Mr. Markham. This laptop belonged to the victim. We have reason to believe he was a private investigator."

If possible, Web became even paler as he sank into a chair. "P... private investigator?"

"Is there any reason someone would be investigating you Mr. Markham?"

"N...not that I'm aware of."

"You're certain."

"Y...yes."

"Thank you, Mr. Markham. Please inform us if you remember anything that might help us wrap up this investigation and please keep the details of this interview to yourself for the time being."

"Y...yes, sir." Web stumbled out the door and leaned on the counter in the entrance hall for a moment before joining the others.

"I'd say that man is shaken up, Dodson."

"His privacy seems to be pretty important to him."

"I'd like to know what's on that laptop that he is so afraid we'll find. I'll need a warrant to find out though."

"I'll call the judge if you want."

"Let's wait and see what turns up with the rest of our interviews. I need a change of pace from the Hollywood set. Send in Mr. Locke next."

Travis Locke quietly walked into the office.

"Please, sit down Mr. Locke," Wade said indicating the chair across from the desk.

Mr. Locke didn't answer.

"Mr. Locke?"

"Why is my case in here?"

"We've collected everything that we think might be important to our investigation. Your case was locked. We'd like for you to open it."

"Why?"

Wade sighed, "There is something missing from the victim. We're trying to locate it. It could be the answer we need.

"What are you looking for?"

"I'm not at liberty to say. Please open the case."

"I'd rather not."

"We can get a warrant if necessary, Mr. Locke."

"You must understand that what is in that case is very old and very delicate."

"I'll allow you to handle the contents. We'll just observe."

Mr. Locke sighed as he pulled a pair of white gloves and a key from his pocket. He put the gloves on and inserted the key into the lock. He slowly opened the case and carefully removed the contents. There were no media cards or any other evidence in the container.

"Thank you, Mr. Locke. I'm sorry for the inconvenience."

Mr. Locke stared at him clearly still annoyed.

"Do you recognize anything else on that table?"

"No, I can't say that I do."

"Do you recognize the man in this photo?"

"No."

"Does the name Sam Hawk mean anything to you?"

"I can't say that it does."

"I'd like you to look at the photos on this laptop."

Travis Locke looked at the pictures with increasing confusion. "I don't understand. What does this mean?"

"We believe the victim was a private investigator. This is his laptop. Do you know of anyone who might be investigating you?"

Mr. Locke blanched and looked at the photos again, "No, I can't say that I do."

"Please, sit down, Mr. Locke. I have few more questions."

"What else do you want to know?" he asked as he sat down.

"How did you come to be at the inn, Mr. Locke?"

"I heard about it on the news the other night. I thought it might be a nice place to visit."

"On the news?

"Yes, the story was about the bodies found near here. I'd be very interested to see what was discovered, Sheriff. I work in the archeology department at the university."

"I see. We may have time to discuss it after this over."

"Thank you. I'd appreciate it."

"When did you get here, Mr. Locke?"

"It was probably between seven-thirty and seven forty-five Friday night. I drove over from Lubbock when I got off work."

"Did you attend the wedding reception last night?"

"Yes, I did. It was a nice little party."

"What time did you leave?"

"I went upstairs at ten o'clock so I could see the news."

"What did you do after that?"

"I watched Leno's monologue and then went to bed."

"Did you hear or see anything that will give us a clue in this case?"

"I don't know if it means anything, but I got up to use the restroom during the night and thought I heard voices outside."

"Do you know what time that was?"

"I believe it was around two-thirty this morning."

"Do you know who was talking?"

"No, I don't. I was too sleepy to care. I shuffled back to bed and was sound asleep again."

"Thank you, Mr. Locke. If you think of anything else that might help us, please let us know. Please, don't discuss this interview with anyone until the interviews have been completed.

"Yes, sir. Don't forget about those bodies," Mr. Locke said as he closed the door.

"He's a strange man," Dodson commented.

"I wonder what that case is all about," Wade pondered aloud. "Oh well, let's get this last interview done. Send in Miss Rockwood."

Rachel Rockwood entered the office as if she were playing the part of the dumb but loveable character in a play.

Dodson rolled his eyes as she passed. Sheriff Adams had to stifle a grin.

"Please, sit down, Miss Rockwood. I have a few questions to ask you."

"Call me Rachel. Isn't this exciting?"

The sheriff chose to ignore the comment and said, "I understand you arrived with Mr. Powell and Mr. Markham on Thursday evening. Is that correct?"

She nodded. "I'm going to be playing Lizzie in their new movie. I've been watching her. I know exactly how I'm going to play the part."

She stood and moved around the room pretending to answer the phone and greet guests. Had Wade not known better, he would have thought it was Lizzie until he looked at Rachel's face.

"That's very good. Please, sit down Miss Rockwood."

Rachel beamed at the sheriff as she sat down.

"I understand that you attended the wedding reception last night. Do you recall what time you left?"

"It was around midnight after the party guests left. They were all so nice. We just couldn't refuse an autograph or posing for a picture."

"I see." Wade hesitated to ask, "What did you do then?"

"Monty and I went to bed."

"Did you hear or see anything during the night that might help us solve this case."

"No, I didn't. I had a bit too much to drink and went right to sleep. I did wake up once and wondered where Monty had gone. He must have been in the restroom because he was there when I woke up this morning."

"Do you recognize any of the items on the table behind me?"

"No, I don't. Should I? Is the murder weapon over there?"

"I'd like for you to look at this photo. Do you recognize the man?"

"Ohhhh, is this the dead man? No, I don't know him. He's handsome. Or should I say was?"

"Does the name Sam Hawk mean anything to you?"

"No," she giggled.

"Do you think his name is funny?"

"Oh, I was only thinking that would be a good name for a police officer or private investigator in a crime drama."

Wade cleared his throat, "I'd like for you to look at the photos on this laptop."

"Okie Dokie."

Rachel scrolled through the pictures. She stopped and looked at some then scrolled through them again. The dumb but loveable character began to disappear as she realized she and the other guests were being watched. She looked up at the sheriff questioningly.

"We believe the victim was a private investigator. This laptop was found in his car. Do you have any idea why someone would be investigating you or anyone here at the inn?"

"No, I don't. But I do think some of these people are not what they seem."

"What do you mean?"

"Excuse me, Sheriff," Lodge interrupted. "Dr. Hughes is calling."

"I need to take that call, Miss Rockwood. You may go for now. We'll discuss this again soon."

"Thank you, Sheriff." Rachel stood and left the room.

"What did you find Doc?"

"Time of death was between two and four this morning. There were no abrasions or bruises other than the obvious blow to his head. The wound matches the size and shape of the rock. He must have been lying in that position when he was struck. What's interesting is that the blow didn't kill him. He was knocked unconscious, and then he drowned lying there in the pool."

"So in your opinion we're still looking for one killer?"

"There is no evidence that more than one person was involved."

"Thanks, Doc."

As Wade hung up the phone, Dodson snapped his own cell phone shut.

"Dan and Megan Hayes are set up for interviews later this afternoon," he told the sheriff.

"We need to keep them separated. Megan is a live wire."

"I've heard that, sir."

"Has the search of the inn and the grounds been completed?"

"Yes. We haven't found anything else."

"Let's pack up. Return the items on the table to their owners. I'll go talk with the folks in the dining room one more time before we leave."

Dodson prepared to return the items as Sheriff Adams walked to the dining room.

SIXTEEN

"Ladies and gentlemen, we have finished our preliminary investigation. You are free to return to your rooms and move about the inn as usual. I must ask that you stay here at the inn or on the grounds until our investigation is complete."

"What about our belongings, Sheriff?"

"Your personal property will be returned before we leave. I have more interviews to conduct in town. Please, call my office if anything comes to mind that you think we should know."

Lizzie walked to the door with the sheriff. "Have you learned anything useful?" she asked.

"Only bits and pieces. We need to figure out how they fit the puzzle. I'll be out here again tomorrow unless something turns up before then."

"Okay, thank you."

The guests were gathered in the dining room and speculated about the murdered man while the Fletcher women went about their daily chores. Lois was in the office answering the phone. Ellen and Lizzie prepared the evening meal. James hovered in the background keeping silent watch. He was concerned about the safety of his family and his guests.

"I wonder which of us was being investigated," Monty pondered.

"It could have been any of us," Web replied.

"Or all of us."

"Why do you say that Mr. Locke?" Ann asked.

"There were photos of each one of us including the Fletchers."

"Maybe someone hired him to investigate the inn," Monty offered.

"Maybe he didn't know what the person he was investigating looked like," Ann added.

"He would probably know if it was a man or woman he was investigating," Web countered.

"He could have been hired to watch and photograph everyone. He may not have known why," Ann replied.

"It's another of those strange things that have been going on here," Rachel said looking around the room.

"What strange things?" Lizzie asked. Everyone else looked at her in surprise.

"People have been doing odd things. Some people have been in places where they shouldn't be. Other's pretended to read an upside-down book while watching everyone else. Someone has been sneaking in and out of the office. Someone has been walking along the creek pacing like a pirate looking for buried treasure. But the oddest thing was seeing lights going on in rooms when everyone was downstairs." Rachel stopped and paused for effect.

Everyone had been paying close attention but seemed to dismiss her monologue as everyday happenings that probably meant nothing. Only the Fletchers took her seriously. They had recently been experiencing enough strange things to last them a life time.

The forensics work began in earnest once the sheriff and his men got back to town. Fingerprints were analyzed. Signatures were compared to the handwriting on the note. Backgrounds were checked. Evidence was examined and reexamined. The interviews were discussed.

It was during that discussion that Dodson said, "Wade, I had the feeling that all of them were holding back information."

"I had that impression, too. Maybe the background checks will give us an idea. Are they finished yet?"

"Not yet. It shouldn't take much longer."

There was a knock on the office door. Lodge opened the door and said, "Dan Hayes is here."

"Send him in," Wade answered. Then, to Dodson he said, "Let me know when those background checks are finished."

"Yes, sir."

Dan walked into the office with a mixture of curiosity and apprehension on his face. Wade stood and shook hands with him and said, "Sit down, Dan. How are you doing?"

"I'm doing okay considering. Is this about Megan?"

"No, it isn't. There was a body found at the inn this morning."

"What!" Dan was clearly flabbergasted. "It wasn't Lizzie was it?"

Wade was surprised. "Why would you think it was Lizzie?"

Dan hesitated a moment before answering, "Megan has been pretty vocal about hating Lizzie. I thought she might have hurt her."

"It wasn't Lizzie or any of the Fletchers."

Dan gave an audible sigh of relief. Wade slid the picture of the victim across the desk for Dan to see. "Do you recognize this man?"

"No. Who is he?"

"His name was Sam Hawk. Does that name mean anything to you?"

"No."

"He was a private investigator. We think he was investigating someone at the inn. Look at these," Wade said as he turned the laptop for Dan to see.

Dan examined the pictures in silence. He looked at Wade when he had finished.

"Do you have any ideas?" Wade asked.

"Megan would be my first thought, but I don't know how she could afford to hire an investigator."

"We're trying to find out who hired him. When was the last time you were at the inn?"

"Friday afternoon. I had the weekend off."

"Where were you this weekend?"

Dan stared at the sheriff for moment before he said, "I've been at my folks place working cattle all weekend. I came directly here when we finished today."

"I'm getting fingerprints from everyone associated with the inn. I'll need yours and your signature so that we can eliminate them from those we've collected at the crime scene."

Dan looked surprised but didn't argue, "Is there any reason I shouldn't go to work tomorrow?"

"No. The Fletchers will need your help. They have a house full of frightened and worried guests."

Lodge tapped on the door and opened it enough to put his head through, "Megan Hayes and her mother are here."

"Show Dan out the back way. I'll bring them in as soon as Dan is out of sight. Thanks for coming in Dan. We hope to get this all cleared up soon."

"I hope so, too."

As soon as Dan was gone, Wade invited Megan and Roxanne into his office. They sat nervously while Wade took his seat.

"Sheriff, is this about the restraining orders? Megan hasn't been out of my sight," Roxanne said.

"No, ma'am. It isn't. I just want to ask you a few questions. Do you know this man?"

Megan glanced at the photo and shrugged, "I don't know him."

Roxanne stared at it for a moment and frowned in thought, "I've seen him at Allsup's."

"Recently?"

"He was in last week. He bought a lot of junk food."

"Do you know his name?"

"No. He barely spoke, and he always paid cash."

"Does the name Sam Hawk ring a bell?"

Both women shook their heads.

"This man was found dead at the inn this morning."

Roxanne said, "Oh no!"

Megan sat up in her chair paying close attention, now. "I'll bet Lizzie did it!"

Wade ignored her. "The man was a private investigator. Can you think of any reason why someone would hire an investigator to watch the inn?"

Megan fidgeted, apparently bored with the conversation. Wade showed them the photos on the laptop. Neither had anything to add although Roxanne looked at her daughter out of the corner of her eye.

"I'll need your fingerprints and signature before you leave, Megan."

"Why? I haven't done anything. You can't have my fingerprints," Megan raged.

"I can get a court order, or I can arrest you for suspicion of murder," Wade answered calmly.

"You can't do that!"

"I can, and I will," Wade replied.

"Is she a suspect, Sheriff?" Roxanne quietly asked.

"Some of these photos and the restraining order make her a prime suspect. If Megan is innocent, she has nothing to worry about."

"Someone has been with her every minute since she was released from the hospital. She couldn't have gone out without my knowledge. Let me talk to her."

Wade walked out of his office. Roxanne spent some time talking and finally convinced Megan to be fingerprinted before they left the office.

"Thank you, Mrs. Ford. We'll be in touch."

Roxanne smiled meekly at the sheriff and followed Megan out the door.

"Run these prints along with the others," he told one of his deputies. *I wonder if Megan has managed to sneak out of her mother's house,* Wade mused.

"The background checks are finished," Dodson said as he placed a stack of papers on the desk in front of Wade. "We couldn't find anything on the Wainrite woman. Not even a driver's license."

"Nothing at all? That's unusual. Maybe she's using an alias. Keep checking. Something has to turn up somewhere. I'll look through these in a bit. What else have you got?"

"The hair and blood did belong to the victim. He's been positively identified, but we still don't know who hired him. His balance in his bank account has remained between eight hundred and a thousand dollars for the past twelve months. There have been no deposits or expenditures in that account for two months and no charges made on his credit cards. He was either paid in cash or was to be paid after the job was finished. We've made several phone calls to his office, but there has been no answer. We'll try again in the morning."

Dodson continued, "None of the signatures we collected match the handwriting on the note. It looks like it came from the pad in the foyer. There was only a partial print on it. We're still trying to find a match. The fingerprints we collected at the inn were consistent with the people working and staying at the inn. There were a few that belonged to the party guests the night before. There were no prints found on the rock."

"Was there anything unexpected found in the car?"

"Only that the memory cards we found were blank. He must have erased them after loading the contents onto the laptop," Dodson answered.

"I'm still betting someone has the missing memory card at the inn. Why would he have the camera but no card? It doesn't make sense," Wade puzzled.

"There was a partial bag of junk food and assorted trash from local restaurants in his car," Dodson added.

"Roxanne Ford said she had seen him in Allsup's. Did anyone else who was interviewed recognize him?"

"Baker is outside. I'll have him come in." Baker entered the office with his notes in hand.

"How did the interviews go?" Wade asked Baker.

"Most didn't recognize him, but there were some who said they had seen him at various places. Several said that he was standoffish when they tried to initiate a conversation with him. No one knew his name. He was seen in town last week."

"That doesn't help much does it? Thanks, Baker. Go home and get some rest."

"Yes, sir. See you in the morning."

"Dodson, let's go over these background checks, and then we'll go home."

The two men read the background checks, discussed them, and made notes. They had suspected those interviewed had been hiding something. They were still surprised by some of the information they found.

"We'll go out there first thing in the morning and interview those folks again. Let's get some rest. Maybe the answer will come to us in our dreams," Wade said jokingly.

The men said goodnight and drove to their respective homes. Wade couldn't help thinking about the case as he lay down for the night. *Why is the FBI watching Lizzie?*

SEVENTEEN

The sheriff and his men arrived at eight o'clock simultaneously with Dan Hayes and the Fletchers.

"Good morning. Anything new," James asked as they went inside.

"Only more questions," Wade answered. "We need to interview everyone again."

The phone began to ring in the office.

"The guests won't be down for at least an hour," Ellen told him.

"We'll interview the four of you first if you don't mind. We'll try not to disrupt your work."

The phone in the office kept ringing.

"Lizzie must be in the kitchen. I'll go help her," Ellen said as she left the room.

"I'll be with you as soon as I get Dan started," James told Wade as he and Dan walked out onto the front porch.

"I guess that leaves me to answer that phone. Excuse me," Lois said opening the office door.

The sheriff and his deputies were waiting in the foyer for James to return when they were startled by a scream coming from the office.

They hurried inside to find Lois standing in front of the desk with her hands over her face, crying.

"No, no, no, no," she repeated.

The three men looked at the desk. The woman sitting there appeared to have fallen asleep while at work. Her red hair covered her face. It was clear to the men that she wasn't sleeping.

"Dodson take Mrs. Fletcher out of here. Lodge, keep everyone out of this room, especially the Fletchers. They don't need to see this." The two men obeyed instantly. Wade tried to clear the lump that had formed in his throat and took out his cell phone. After calling his team, he called Dr. Hughes.

"Doc, you're needed at the inn. We've found another body." He paused, listening to the doctor, "No, this time the victim is in the office."

Ellen had been walking back toward the foyer when she heard the scream. She rushed to see what had happened. When she saw Lois, she asked, "What's wrong?"

Lois couldn't speak in her grief. She looked at Ellen, shook her head, and sobbed.

"Lizzie! Lizzie!" Ellen screamed as she ran toward the office. Dodson and Lodge were doing their best to keep her out. James came inside and asked, "What's going on in here?"

"It's Lizzie," Lois sobbed.

James looked at the two men guarding the door. "We're terribly sorry, sir," Dodson said.

Tears ran down James face as he said, "I want to see my little girl."

Wade came out of the office. He tried to hide his emotions as he said, "I'm so sorry. You don't want to see her like this. Let's go to the dining room and sit down. Dr. Hughes will be here soon."

Lodge stood guard at the office door while the others reluctantly made their way to the dining room.

The guests were awakened by the noise and began to come downstairs.

"What's happening?"

"What's wrong?"

"What's going on?"

"Who's screaming?"

"Please, make your way to the dining room," Wade told them. "We'll tell you what we know there." He waited for everyone to take a seat.

"I'm sorry to tell you that another murder has been committed here. My team has been called and will be here shortly. I have some questions while we wait."

"Was it another John Doe, Sheriff?" Locke asked.

"No, it wasn't."

"Was another body found in the pool?" Ms. Wainrite queried.

"No, ma'am," Wade said. He took a deep breath before continuing.

"We won't know for sure until the medical examiner gets here, but" Wade paused as if unable to continue, "it appears to be Lizzie Fletcher."

The guests gasped in surprise and gathered around the grieving family. The Fletchers sobbed all the more.

"Who would want to hurt Lizzie?" Monty asked.

The patio door opened. The woman was startled when she saw so many people in the dining room. She hadn't expected anyone to be downstairs so early. She looked around the room. *What has upset everyone and why were they huddled around my family?* Dodson was looking at her as if he'd seen a ghost.

"What's wrong? What's happened?" Lizzie asked.

Everyone looked at her in disbelief. Tears of sorrow quickly changed to those of joy and relief. Her family rushed to her almost knocking her off her feet.

"You're alive!"

"It wasn't you!"

"I thought it was you!"

"What are you talking about?" Lizzie asked confused.

"There's been another murder," Wade said relieved that Lizzie had not been the woman found in the office.

Monty stared. He smiled when he realized Lizzie was alive and well. "You're alive!" he said.

"Since Lizzie is here, who was killed?" Locke asked.

"The victim is a woman with red hair," Wade said.

"Rachel? It can't be! She's still upstairs. She has to be," Monty exclaimed as he went upstairs in search of Rachel. Moments later he returned. "She isn't up there. Maybe she went for a walk."

"It's likely that the victim is Miss Rockwood," Wade said. "I'm sorry."

"It can't be! It just can't!" Monty said as he sank into a chair.

"How did it happen?" Web asked.

"Sheriff, the team has arrived," Lodge informed him.

"I'd rather not say anything, Mr. Markham, until the doctor has finished his examination. I came here this morning to interview each of you again. Now, I have more questions than I anticipated. I'll interview each of you in turn on the patio," Wade said.

"Isn't the office a more private place?"

"Not today Ms. Wainrite. The office is occupied. Mr. Fletcher, I'll talk with you first so that the ladies can tend to your guests. "

James nodded and followed Wade to the patio.

"I'm sorry about the mistake earlier James. It did look like Lizzie in there."

James swallowed hard. "I'm glad I didn't see the body. Mom's description was bad enough. I don't know what I would have done."

"What happened after we left yesterday?" Wade asked.

"The guests discussed the murder. They went upstairs after dinner. We helped with the clean up and went home."

"What were the guests discussing?"

"They were speculating about who was being investigated and why," James replied.

"Did anyone say anything that might give us a clue?"

"Rachel said something about strange things happening here?"

"What kinds of strange things?"

"I don't remember exactly. I remember thinking they weren't all that strange."

"Was there any indication that another murder was about to happen?"

"Not that I noticed."

"There were no threats made toward Lizzie or Rachel last night?"

James shook his head, "None last night."

Wade was suddenly alert. "Have there been threats in the past?"

James sighed, "It probably has nothing to do with this, but the family was threatened."

"When? How?"

"It was shortly after the bodies were found by the creek. There was an anonymous letter in the mail. It said we had disturbed mother earth by removing what she had claimed. It went on to say that mother earth will seek her vengeance."

"Was it handwritten or typed?" Wade asked.

"It was typed."

"What did you do with it?"

"I put it away so that Ellen or Mom wouldn't see it. I didn't want them to worry over someone's idea of a joke."

"I'd like to see that letter. Why didn't you mention it before?"

"I didn't think it had anything to do with that man's death. I thought it was someone playing a prank."

"Is there anything else that I should know?" Wade asked.

"Not that I can think of at the moment. Do you think Lizzie was the intended victim last night?"

"It's possible. We won't know for sure until we learn more. I believe the two deaths are somehow connected."

James sat deep in thought for a moment. Then he said, "Hawk wasn't connected to us or to Lizzie. I'm sure of it. I'll get that letter for you."

"Thanks. I'd like to see Ellen now."

James nodded and went to call Ellen.

Ellen sat down and waited for Wade's first question.

"What happened after we left here last night?" Wade asked.

Ellen's answer was practically identical to her husband's.

"Did you hear Rachel say something about strange things happening?"

"No, I didn't. I must have been in the kitchen."

"Did you notice a threat of any kind toward Lizzie or Rachel?"

"No."

Wade felt there was something she was holding back. "Has anyone threatened Lizzie or the family recently?" he asked.

Ellen hesitated before answering, "I hate to say this. She isn't well and was in the hospital at the time."

"Who?"

"Megan Hayes."

"What about her?"

"I was answering the phones here the day that Lizzie and Drake filed the restraining orders. Megan phoned shortly before Lizzie got home. She must have thought she was talking to Lizzie. She said that a restraining order wouldn't stop her. She said she had seen them together. She said that I would pay for taking Drake and Dan from her. Then she hung up. I thought patients weren't allowed access to phones in the psychiatric ward. How could she have seen them while she was in the hospital in Wichita Falls?"

"Hmmm, I'll check on that. Does anyone else know about the phone call?"

"I didn't tell anyone. I thought she would be in the hospital much longer than she was. I didn't see the point in worrying everyone."

"Why didn't you mention the phone call when you were interviewed before?"

"I thought about it but didn't think it had anything to do with that poor man."

Wade rubbed his temples as if to keep a headache at bay. "Thank you, Ellen. Please, send Lois out to see me."

Lois sat down obviously still shaken by her discovery. Wade asked her the same questions he had asked James and Ellen. Lois had been busy in the kitchen and hadn't heard any of the dinner conversation. She had gone home with her son and daughter-in-law.

"Did you touch anything in the office this morning?"

Her eyes welled up with tears. "The phone stopped ringing before I could answer it. I thought Lizzie had fallen asleep at her desk. I called her name. She didn't answer, so I reached out to give her a little shake. She was so cold."

"That's when you screamed."

Lois nodded.

Wade allowed Lois a few minutes to compose herself. "Did you touch anything else?"

"No."

"Do you know of any threats made toward Lizzie or Rachel?"

Her expression hardened as she said, "There have been no direct threats that I'm aware of. But from time to time treasure hunters show up here looking for that damned gold. People show up with their shovels and their dreams of getting rich. We have to run them off our land. Sometimes they get nasty. I think finding those bodies by the creek might have stirred things up again."

"I'm familiar with that story. People still believe there is gold to be found here?"

"Some do."

"So you think someone is looking for buried treasure and is willing to kill for it."

"I'm just telling you about a possible threat."

"Thank you, Lois. Send Lizzie out now please."

"Stop them before anyone else dies, Wade."

"Yes, ma'am."

Lizzie sat down and tried to relax. She was unnerved by Rachel's death.

"Tell me what happened after we left," Wade said.

Lizzie told him about the conversations.

"Anything else?"

"Rachel said something odd."

"What did she say?"

"She said the murder was another of the strange things going on here. I asked her what she meant. She listed several things and looked at each of the guests in turn."

"Do you remember what she said?"

Lizzie closed her eyes in an effort to remember. "She said someone was watching people while pretending to read a book. Someone was in places they shouldn't be. She said someone was sneaking in and out of the office. She also said something about someone pacing like a pirate along the creek. The comment that bothered me most was lights going on in rooms when everyone was downstairs."

"So you think it's possible that someone was here who shouldn't have been."

"Exactly," Lizzie said.

"Do you remember who she looked at when she said those things?"

"No, I don't. I'm sorry."

"What happened after that?"

"The guests went upstairs, and my family went home for the night. I went into my office to check messages. I returned a few personal phone calls before going to my room. I tried to read but couldn't relax. I couldn't stop thinking about the man in the pool. I went to the kitchen to make myself some hot tea and went back to my room, but I was still restless. I thought maybe a hot shower would help me relax. I showered until the water started to get cold. After that, I put on my pajamas and fell into bed. The last thing I remember before going to sleep was the crickets chirping outside my window."

"Did you see or hear anything?"

"No, the house was quiet."

"What did you do this morning?" Wade asked.

"I overslept this morning. It was seven forty-five when I got up. I got dressed as quickly as I could and went to the pantry to decide what to make for breakfast. I set out some things to start preparing. I noticed the clock in the dining room wasn't working. I couldn't find any batteries in here, so I went to the cellar to find some. I looked for several minutes before I found them. When I came back, everyone was in the dining room."

"You didn't see or hear anything unusual?"

"Nothing other than seeing my family grieving my death."

"Have there been any threats against you or your family that we don't already know about?"

"No."

"Lizzie, why does the FBI have a file on you?" Wade asked watching her closely.

Lizzie stared at him for a moment lost in his eyes. "They have a file on me?" she asked.

"Yes," he said and continued watching her.

"The only contact I've had with them was when an agent came to see me."

"Why?"

Lizzie reluctantly told him about Rob.

"You don't consider this man to be a threat?"

"Not anymore. He died."

"Who was the agent you talked to?"

"Greg Jenkins. Do you think I was the target?"

"It appears that you were," he said as he reached out and took her hand. "Don't worry. We'll have a security detail round the clock until we find who's responsible."

"The team is here, Sheriff," Dodson interrupted.

"If you'll excuse me, Lizzie, I'll leave you to attend to your guests."

Wade met the team at the door and led them into the office. They began their work immediately. It appeared that Rachel had been strangled from behind with the cord of a lamp found lying nearby on the floor. Monty was called to identify her body before it was taken for autopsy.

"Do you know why Rachel was in the office?"

Monty answered as if he was remembering a nightmare. "No. She said she couldn't sleep. She was going downstairs to borrow a movie. I asked her to get a book instead so that I could concentrate while reading the script. She went downstairs, and I must have fallen asleep. I thought she was in the bathroom when I woke up."

"Do you have any idea who might have killed her or why?"

"No. I can't understand it."

"We've been checking the backgrounds of everyone here at the inn. You had quite a large debt built up. Then suddenly, it was paid in full. How do you explain that?"

"I like to gamble. I hit it big one night and paid off all my debts," Monty said with a shrug.

"Most people aren't that lucky."

"I was hot that night. I couldn't lose."

"I understand that you have connections with some bad people. Could they have been the source of your good fortune?"

Monty paled but didn't answer.

"How long have you been seeing Rachel?"

"We've been together five or six months," Monty answered seemingly relieved that the questions were no longer about him.

"Did you know that her real name was Tammie Welch and that she was reported as a runaway when she was fifteen?"

"Yes, she told me. Her father used to beat her and her mother. She ran away after her mother died. She was always afraid he would find her."

"According to her records, she recently turned twenty-one."

Monty stared at him in disbelief. "She told me she was twenty-six."

"It appears she changed more than her name. I'd say she had some cosmetic surgery to change her appearance," Wade said as he showed him the police file photo.

"Are you sure this is Rachel?"

"The prints match. We'll compare DNA to confirm her identity."

"Do you think her father found her?"

"I don't know. We'll be looking into that possibility. If you think of anything else we should know, don't hesitate to tell me or one of my deputies."

"Am I free to go?"

"For now, I may have to talk with you again as more evidence is discovered."

Monty walked away visibly shaken. After the body was removed, Wade sent Dodson to find Lizzie. When she entered the office Wade said, "I'd like for you to look around the room. Tell me if anything is missing or out of place."

Lizzie carefully looked at her surroundings. "This book wasn't here last night. A small reading lamp is missing. It should be sitting on that file cabinet. I'm certain that I turned the computer off before going to my room last night. Everything else is where it should be."

"Do you know who owns the book?"

"We do. It's part of the inn library."

"Do you know who was reading it?"

"No, I'm sorry. Ms. Wainrite has done a lot of reading, but I don't know if she was reading this one."

"Where does this door lead?"

"To my room."

"Was it locked last night?"

"It doesn't lock."

"Anyone could have used this door last night."

Lizzie looked at him wide eyed. "Yes, I suppose so."

"Do any of the guests know that it's here?"

"I gave Web, Rachel, and Monty a tour of the inn when they arrived. Monty already knew about it. He stayed in my room when he was injured. I stayed in here so that I would be close by if he needed help."

"Do your other guests know about it?"

"I don't know."

"Thanks, Lizzie. I may have more questions later."

When Lizzie left the room, Wade said, "Dodson, let's try to piece together what we know so far. Rachel Rockwood came downstairs to find a book to read. Maybe she chose that book on the desk. She came to the office rather than going back upstairs. Why would she do that?"

Wade stood in thought for a moment.

"You were saying sir," Dodson said interrupting Wade's thoughts.

Wade came out of his reverie. "Were the lights on when the body was discovered?"

"I don't recall," Dodson replied.

"If the lights were on when Rachel came in, she would have seen anyone already in the room. She knew that person. She sat down at the computer. She felt no alarm that the person was behind her. What was she doing at the computer? Did she turn it on, or was it already on when she sat down?"

"Someone could have crept up behind her using that door," Dodson pointed out.

"That's another possibility."

Wade continued, "If the lights were off, someone could possibly hide without being seen or could have come in unnoticed through that door. Dodson seal the adjoining door to this room for now. I'll have Lodge stand guard at the office door. I'll talk to Lizzie about going through this computer. I'll finish the rest of the interviews on the patio. Bag that book, and dust it for prints. Maybe the killer left it there rather than Miss Rockwood."

"Yes, sir. Have you ever read this book, *Death on the Nile?*"

"No, but I've seen a movie version. It was pretty good. I enjoyed it."

EIGHTEEN

Wade saw Lois as he walked to the dining room. "Just the person I need to see," he said. "Were the lights on or off when you went into the office this morning?"

"I'm not sure. I didn't turn them on. There was enough light in the room to see. I just went in and walked to the phone."

"Wade," James called.

"Thank you, Lois. What do you have James?"

"I brought this for you to see," James said handing him an envelope.

"Thanks. I'll get someone started on this right away. Have you seen Lizzie?"

"She's probably in the kitchen. I'll tell her you need to see her."

"I'd appreciate that, thank you. Dodson, add this to the list of things to be dusted for prints."

Wade took out his cell phone while he waited for Lizzie. The phone rang twice at his office before someone answered, "Sheriff's office."

"Baker, have someone check all incoming calls to the inn for the past month. I'm particularly interested in any that might have come from the psychiatric ward at the hospital, Megan Hayes, or anyone connected with her. I also want to know who visited her in the hospital and when. See if you can find out if she managed to slip away from those who were supposed to be keeping an eye on her after her release."

"Yes, sir. She was home all night last night and so was Dan Hayes."

"All right, let me know when you have something."

"Yes, sir."

"Wade, did you need to see me?" Lizzie asked as he hung up the phone.

"Yes, I need your permission to examine the contents of your computer. Someone turned it on last night. We might be able to find something useful."

"There isn't much on it other than business records."

"If someone was sneaking in and out of your office, your computer may have been used."

Lizzie pondered that thought as they made their way to the office.

"Guests don't have access to my files. I have a guest account set up in case the WIFI isn't working."

"Let's have a look at that guest account then," Wade suggested.

Lizzie opened the guest account so that Wade could examine it. "I'll be in the kitchen if you need me," she said and left the office.

Wade perused the guest files on the computer for a few minutes. No one had saved anything there. He opened the internet browser and a chat window opened. The text read *I won't be able to chat with you for a while. I'm grounded for two weeks.*

Wade checked the browsing history. Someone had been chatting on the office computer nightly since Thursday evening. He called his office again. "Baker, find out who has been chatting with someone on this computer." He provided the necessary information and hung up. *Rachel did see someone sneaking in and out of the office*, he thought.

"Sheriff," Dodson said when he opened the office door. "The

prints on the letter belong to Megan Hayes. There are two sets of prints on the book. One set belongs to Miss Rockwood and the other to Ms. Wainrite.

"Send Ms. Wainrite to the patio, please."

Ann Wainrite appeared to be composed as she sat across from the sheriff.

"Ms. Wainrite, what did you do after dinner?"

"I borrowed a book and went upstairs. I read for a while then went to sleep."

"Do you read only in your room?"

"I like to read anywhere, especially if it's a quiet place."

"Do you spend a lot of time reading?"

"Yes, I do. It's my way of escaping."

"What are you trying to escape, Ms. Wainrite?"

"What do you mean?" she answered warily.

"There is no record of Ann Wainrite to be found. No bank accounts, no credit cards, not even a driver's license."

"I prefer to use cash, so I have no need for a bank account or credit cards. I don't drive or own a car. I either walk or hire a cab."

"Where do you get your money?"

"I inherited from a neighbor that had no family. I looked after him when he was ill."

"I see," Wade said unconvinced.

"Do you recognize this?" Wade asked holding an evidence bag containing the book found in the office.

"I borrowed that book the night I arrived. I finished it that evening and returned it."

"This book was found beside Miss Rockwood's body. Do you have any idea how it happened to be there?"

"Miss Rockwood probably borrowed it."

"Why do you think she borrowed it?"

"I was reading it by the pool. She asked if it was a good book and said she would like to read it when I finished."

"Thank you, Ms. Wainrite. You may return to the dining room. Dodson, have Mr. Locke join us next."

Wade pondered the conversation with Ann Wainrite while he waited for Mr. Locke. She was lying. They would have to keep digging to find her true identity.

Travis Locke cleared his throat. "You wanted to see me, Sheriff?"

"Yes, Mr. Locke. Please sit down." Wade continued as Locke took his seat, "What did you do after dinner last night?"

"I borrowed a movie and went upstairs. I couldn't hear most of it. That young couple across the hall were having a whale of an argument. I went to bed when they settled down."

"Did you hear what was said?"

"Couldn't help but hear even with a pillow over my head."

"What were they arguing about?"

"She said he wasn't paying enough attention to her. He said he was busy working on the movie. She called him a liar and said he was too busy chasing after Lizzie or wandering around in places he shouldn't be. They finally closed the door, and I couldn't make out what was being said. It wasn't long until one of them went downstairs."

"Did you hear anyone else leave or come back upstairs?"

"No, I went to sleep."

"We've checked the backgrounds of everyone here at the inn. We found something interesting while looking into your background."

Locke shifted in his chair.

"You don't work with the archeology department of any university. You were employed as a custodian. You were fired six months ago."

"I was laid off not fired. I worked in the building that housed the archeology department."

"Are you employed now?"

"I'm still looking for a job."

"Why are you here, Mr. Locke?"

"I've always found the field of archeology fascinating. I heard the story on the news and decided to come see for myself. How often will a man like me get the chance to see something like that?"

"Have you ever heard the local legend about buried treasure out here?"

"No, I can't say that I have."

"Have you seen the grave site?"

Locke hesitated before answering, "Yes, I have. It was disappointing to find it was already closed. I would have liked to have seen what was found there."

"It will have to wait until this case is over. Thank you, Mr. Locke."

"What do you think?" Dodson asked.

"I think there's more to his visit here than he's telling us. Let's see Markham next."

Wade's cell phone rang. "I have some news for you," Baker said. Wade raised an eyebrow as he listened. Finally, he said, "Get a warrant, and get it out here. We'll handle things on this end. Oh, you already have it? Excellent work! Bring the files with the information you've found, too." He hung up and said, "I need everyone in the dining room before interviewing Markham."

Dodson and Lodge asked the Fletchers and their guests to assemble again in the dining room. They were waiting impatiently when the Sheriff stood to address them.

"Ladies and gentlemen, we have some information to share with you." He held up the evidence bag containing the note paper. "This note was found near the body of Sam Hawk. We believe it was torn from the notepad kept at the check in desk in the lobby. The handwriting on this note doesn't match anyone's handwriting here. However, it is a match to Hawk's handwriting."

Wade paused for a moment watching the faces of the people in front of him. "I believe he wrote this note and left it for a specific person to find."

"So he was inside the inn," Lizzie said.

"Yes, he was. It was probably when there was a lot of activity and no one would have noticed."

"Didn't Rachel say something about lights going on in rooms when everyone was downstairs?" James asked.

"Yes, she did!" Monty said.

"Did she say which room?" Wade asked.

Everyone shook their heads. She hadn't mentioned which rooms.

"It's possible then that Hawk came into the inn, wrote this note, delivered it to one of the rooms upstairs, and left without being noticed. The question now is who found the note?"

Wade looked around the room. No one gave any indication that they had received the note. "We don't know yet who hired Hawk. We should be hearing from his office soon."

"Baker is here, sir," Dodson informed him. Wade gave whispered instructions to Dodson and left the room to meet with Baker.

"Mr. Markham, I'd like to talk with you on the patio, please," Wade said when he returned. The sheriff and Web Markham walked to the patio together.

"Please, sit down, Mr. Markham."

Web was seated comfortably when Wade asked, "What did you do after dinner last night?"

"I went upstairs to work on the screenplay."

Dodson appeared on the patio with Web's laptop.

"I'd like to see that screenplay, Mr. Markham," Wade said as Dodson placed the laptop on the table in front of the sheriff.

"That's private property, my property. You can't invade my privacy."

"We'd rather have your cooperation, but we do have this warrant if necessary," Wade said as he waved the official document in front of Web.

Beads of sweat began to form on Web's face. He took the paper from Wade's hand and groaned as he read it.

Wade smiled inwardly with satisfaction and opened the laptop. The screenplay was in one of the files. There were only half a dozen pages completed. Wade opened other files and looked at the browsing history. He felt physically ill as pornographic photos of very young girls filled the screen.

Webster Markham, I'm placing you under arrest for possession of child pornography. There is also a warrant for your arrest in California. The parents of that fifteen year old girl you've been chatting with every night aren't very happy with you. They've filed charges."

Web broke down and wept openly.

"Before my deputy takes you away, I want you to understand that if I find evidence that you are responsible for these two murders you will have lots of time in prison to write your plays. I have a theory. Would you like to hear it?" Wade asked as Web stared at him.

"I think that little girl's family hired Hawk to find you. You found the note in your room. You met Hawk by the pool. He had photos to prove he'd found you. He wanted money to keep quiet. You killed him to make sure he couldn't talk. Rachel found you in the office that night and saw what you were doing. You strangled her to keep her from exposing your secret."

"I swear I didn't kill anyone. I never saw that P.I. before. Rachel saw me sneaking out of the office one night. I was careful not to be seen after that."

"Take him away, Baker."

Baker cuffed Web and read him his rights. Dodson bagged the laptop for evidence. Baker and Dodson escorted Webster Markham around the inn to the deputy's car. Dodson returned and asked, "What's next?"

Wade read through the files and information that Baker had provided.

"Let's see if we can shake up Montgomery Powell."

Monty sauntered out to the patio. "More questions, Sheriff?" he asked. "I thought you arrested Web."

"Mr. Markham has been arrested on charges unrelated to our current investigation."

"What? What kind of charges?" Monty asked obviously surprised.

"I'm not at liberty to say. Please, sit down."

"I'd rather stand if you don't mind."

Wade nodded. "That's your prerogative." He looked at the actor a moment before saying, "You lied to me."

"When? About what?"

"I've seen that script. There isn't much to read."

Monty shifted his weight.

"I understand that you and Rachel had a loud argument last night. You neglected to tell me about it."

"It was only a little lovers' quarrel. I didn't think it mattered."

"What was the quarrel about?"

"What do women always argue about? I was ignoring her, spending too much time on the script, we're supposed to be on vacation and that sort of thing."

"Had you been ignoring her?"

"No." He paused and after a moment said, "Maybe a little."

"I have a theory that I'd like to share with you. I think you were hiding from someone when you stayed here after your plane crashed. I think you decided to hide here again using the movie as a pretense."

Monty said nothing as Wade continued. "Maybe someone hired Hawk to find you. He left you that note, and you met him at the pool. He had photos to prove your whereabouts, and he wanted money to keep quiet. You killed him instead of paying him off. Maybe that argument with Rachel was more than a little spat. She asked too many questions and saw too much. You followed her when she went downstairs and into the office. Maybe you apologized for the fight. Maybe you didn't. Maybe, when she turned her back, you strangled her."

Monty stood openmouthed for a moment. The he said, "That's

some theory. It's absolutely fascinating, but completely wrong. Have you ever considered writing, Sheriff?"

"Not at all," Wade stared unamused.

"I loved Rachel. I was planning to propose as soon as this divorce is over. I wouldn't, I couldn't hurt her. I never saw that Hawk person before either."

Wade continued to stare but said nothing more.

"Are we finished here, Sheriff?"

"For now." Wade nodded and watched Monty as he stormed back into the house.

"I'd say you hit a nerve," Dodson said after Monty had gone.

"Yes, but which one. Let's see Ms. Wainrite again. Maybe I can crack that icy demeanor."

Ms. Wainrite settled herself in the chair across from the sheriff before asking, "Haven't I answered all of your questions to your satisfaction?"

"I have some new ones for you."

She sighed and said, "Ask if you must."

"We found records of a man by the name of Clark Allen Wainrite. He was married to a woman named Anna. Unfortunately, both are deceased. They had two children. Clark Allen Wainrite Jr. died after being hit by a car at the age of ten. Their daughter is still living. Her name is Cynthia Ann Wainrite. That wouldn't happen to be you would it?"

She only stared at him.

"I'll take that as a yes. Shall I continue?" Wade asked as she looked away. "Cynthia Ann Wainrite married and had two children. Her husband was the late Robert Berkett."

"How did you find out?" she asked meekly.

"We discovered that the FBI had been watching Miss Fletcher. The agent working the case filled us in."

"Agent Jenkins," she said.

"Yes. Why are you here, Mrs. Berkett?"

"That investigation made me realize that my husband was cheating on me. I wanted to believe he had been seduced. I came here to see what the woman was like. I used my maiden name so that I could watch her without raising suspicion."

"How did you find her?"

She signed in at the hospital when she visited Rob. I found her name there. I thought it was fate when one of her business cards was given to me by a friend after Rob's death. I wasn't sure it was the same woman, but I had to find out."

"I'm sorry for your loss. According to Agent Jenkins, you had no idea what was happening."

"No, I didn't."

"I have a story to tell you."

"A story?" Mrs. Berkett asked clearly confused.

"There was once a woman who hired Hawk to find the alleged mistress of her late husband. Hawk discovered that the mistress was the proprietor of a little inn. The woman booked a room there. Hawk left a note asking the woman to meet him. He demanded more money. He knew her real identity and knew that she didn't want to be exposed. She had no money because all of her assets were frozen. She needed to protect her identity. In desperation, the woman killed Hawk."

Wade continued as she looked at him stone faced. "I haven't decided on the ending yet because it could go one of two ways. Ending number one is that Rachel saw and talked too much. The woman followed her down stairs, into the office, and strangled her. Ending two is that the woman used the door between Lizzie's room and the office to find who she thought was Lizzie and strangled her."

Wade looked at Mrs. Berkett and said, "What do you think of my story? Which ending do you like best?"

"This is absurd," she said as she stood. "Are you quite finished?"

"For the time being."

Ms. Wainrite also known as Mrs. Berkett stomped back to the dining room.

"I'd say you broke the ice," Dodson said with a grin.

"Okay, let's see what Locke thinks of my story."

Locke took his place across the table from the sheriff. "Did you forget to ask me something, Sheriff?"

"Are you here treasure hunting?"

"I don't know that you would call it treasure hunting."

"There is no gold here, Mr. Locke."

"There are all kinds of treasure, Sheriff."

"I think you're here looking for the gold that is believed to be buried near here. I also think it's possible that Hawk somehow found out about your treasure hunt. Maybe, he wanted a cut, so you killed him. Rachel's comments made you uneasy. She may know too much. You followed her to the office, and you strangled her as soon as you had the opportunity."

"You can't prove any of that."

"No, I can't. At least, not yet."

Locke glared at him and walked away.

Wade had been ignoring the cell phone vibrating at his hip. He answered it after the interview with Locke ended. "Wade Adams," he paused listening. "I'm on my way."

"Dodson, I've got to go back to town. Dr. Hughes has something I need to see. Stay close to Lizzie. She may be in danger. Keep your eyes open for anything that will help us solve this case."

NINETEEN

Wade was deep in thought as he drove back into town. He had gone over every interview and every piece of evidence in his mind. No matter how he looked at it, he couldn't make all the pieces fit. He was worried. He shuddered at the memory of seeing the body he had believed to be Lizzie. There were two people with a possible motive to kill her. One of them was at the inn. The only evidence he had against that suspect were the fingerprints on a book. He decided to stop at his office before going to see Dr. Hughes.

"Hello, Sheriff," Baker greeted him.

"How is Markham doing?"

"He's been blubbering like a baby," Baker replied disgustedly.

"He may have a lot more to cry about when this is over. Do you have anything else on Hawk?"

"I called a friend with the Dallas police department and asked him to find what he could. Hawk didn't have many cases. The few that he did have were divorce cases. He worked out of his apartment and car. He had a sister living in Fort Worth. I talked with her for a little while. She said he was hard up for money. She and her husband had been helping him out when they could. He was hoping to make some cash taking pictures of the celebrities at the inn. He had phoned her the night before he died and told her that he was going to come home with big money."

"Did she know where he was going to get the cash?" Wade asked.

"He wouldn't tell her. She said she had heard that story before and didn't believe him."

"Okay. What else have you got?"

"There aren't any phones in the rooms of the psych ward. The phone call to the inn was made from a cell phone. The phone belongs to Megan's friend Terry Meaker. Terry had been the only visitor other than Megan's mother."

"Where was Megan last night?"

"This report says she was home all night last night."

"What about Dan Hayes?"

"He was home all night, sir. He's an old friend of mine. We played cards and talked until around three this morning. He told me something interesting."

"Oh?"

"He was hired as a handyman but also as protection for Lizzie. She was in some sort of danger, and James didn't want to leave her completely alone while they were on vacation. He was supposed to stay close by at the Fletchers' place when they were away. He planned to stay at their place, but the storm hit before he could get out there. Later, he was told the danger had passed."

"That explains why he was so determined to get to the inn after the storm," Wade said.

"He's worried that the Fletchers, especially Lizzie, are still in danger."

"He isn't the only one. I'm going to see Dr. Hughes. He says he has something that I need to see."

"Before you go, I have one more bit of information you need to hear," Baker said. "Trey, the bartender at the Watering Hole, recognized the photo of Hawk. He was in the bar one night. He was sitting at a table getting cozy with Megan Hayes."

Wade raised an eyebrow. "Did he say when?"

"He wasn't sure but thought it was soon after those bodies were found near the creek."

"Get Megan in here for questioning. I'll be back after I see Dr. Hughes."

Wade had been pondering the new information all the way to the doctor's office. He was still lost in thought when Dr. Hughes met him at the office door.

"I'm sorry to be so mysterious, but I thought you'd want to see this for yourself," the doctor said.

"Lead the way."

Dr. Hughes led the sheriff to the basement. Rachel Rockwood was lying on a table covered with a sheet.

"Miss Rockwood died between ten-thirty last night and twelve-thirty this morning. She died of strangulation as we expected. I found some of her own skin under her nails. That and the scratches on her neck indicate that she tried to pull the cord away. There were also some light colored cotton fibers under her nails. The dressing gown she was wearing was made of satin. She probably scratched her attacker while struggling to get free."

"Can we match those fibers to a suspect?"

"Possibly, but it would take months. I have something to show you that might solve the case much faster," Dr. Hughes replied.

The doctor walked to a nearby cabinet. He returned holding an evidence bag containing a memory card. "This was lodged in her throat," he said.

"In her throat? Do you have any idea how it got there?"

"I don't believe she was forced to swallow it. There was no damage to her lips or tongue. It was probably in her mouth when she was attacked."

"Have you looked at it?"

"My computer here is too old to access the card. I thought you should be the first to see the contents. I'd like to look at it with you if you don't mind."

Wade grinned and said, "All right, follow me back to my office. I hope this has the piece of the puzzle that we need so we can make an arrest."

Wade and Dr. Hughes entered the sheriff's office together. Megan Hayes sat in a chair at Baker's desk.

"Doc, if you'll wait here, I'll be with you as soon as I've finished with Mrs. Hayes."

The doctor sat down at an unoccupied desk as the sheriff led Megan to his office. "Have a seat Mrs. Hayes."

"I'd prefer to be called Miss Ford or Megan."

"Have a seat Megan," Wade said with a bit more authority.

"Why am I here again?"

"I have some things to talk with you about."

"Like what?" Megan asked while she slouched in the chair and picked at her nails.

Wade showed her the letter that James had given him. "This has your prints all over it."

"Oh," she said. "I forgot about that."

"You admit sending it?"

Megan shrugged. "It was only a joke. What's the big deal?"

"How did you manage to call the inn while you were in the hospital?"

"I used Terry's phone."

"Why did you make that call?"

"I don't know. I guess I felt like it."

"This letter and that phone call are considered threats. Since there have been two murders at the inn in past two days...," he paused to let her process her situation.

Megan sat up straight, "What are you saying?"

"There have been two deaths at the inn. You've made multiple threats against Lizzie Fletcher and her family. You were seen talking with the first victim at the Watering Hole. Everything points to you, Megan."

Megan paled and said, "Terry had seen Drake and Lizzie at Dan's place. She saw them together again at the courthouse. She thought I'd want to know and took their picture. She showed me the picture when she came to visit me. I decided to tell Lizzie she wasn't going to get away with taking the men in my life from me. I didn't kill anyone."

"You lied to me. You said you didn't know Sam Hawk."

"What do you want from me?" Megan screamed.

Wade stood, slammed his hands on his desk, and said firmly. "I want the truth, Megan. Your future depends on it."

Megan sighed, "I met him at the bar that night. He was asking questions about the inn. He said he was going to take some pictures of the people there and try to make some money. He was hoping for celebrity shots or some of the bodies being dug up by the creek. I told him that if he could get pictures of Dan cheating on me with Lizzie I'd pay him. I never saw him again."

"Why didn't you tell me this before?"

"I didn't feel like it."

"Do you understand that you are the primary suspect for both murders?"

Megan rolled her eyes, and Wade made a split second decision. He walked around his desk and said, "Megan Ford Hayes, I'm arresting you for the murder of Sam Hawk and Lizzie Fletcher."

Megan stared at him open mouthed as the sheriff used the intercom to call his deputy. "Maddie, read Mrs. Hayes her rights and escort her to the women's lockup."

Maddie returned to join the sheriff and Baker after locking Megan away. "What are we charging her with?" she asked.

Wade answered. "She never asked who the second victim was. She either doesn't care..."

"Or she thinks she knows," Baker interrupted.

"I told her she was being charged for the murder of Hawk and for Lizzie's murder. She still showed no sign that she was innocent. I want someone watching her. Don't let her make a phone call yet. I want to see what's on the media card first. We may have to release her, but we'll know right where to find her if we discover she is responsible for the deaths. Maybe, she'll learn not to threaten people while she's sitting in there."

"Yes, sir," Baker grinned.

"Doctor, let's have a look at this media card."

The two men went to a nearby computer, inserted the media card, and opened the files. They stared at the screen as they scrolled through the photographs.

TWENTY

Wade phoned Dodson before leaving his office. "Ask Lizzie to set up the big screen so that we can project from a laptop onto it. When that is completed, gather everyone into the dining room. Make sure they are seated so that they can see the screen and we can see them. I'll be there in forty-five minutes."

"Yes, sir," Dodson replied and the conversation ended.

"It's ready, Sheriff," Baker informed Wade. He had copied the photos from the media card onto the laptop and put them into a slide show.

"Is someone else here to keep an eye on our guests?" Wade asked.

"Maddie is still here."

"Then you come with me and run the machine. You've gathered a lot of the information and you should be in on this."

"Yes, sir," Baker smiled.

All was ready when the two men returned to the inn. They could feel the tension in the room. Baker set up the laptop while Wade whispered instructions to Dodson and Lodge.

"If I could have your attention please," Wade began. "I've been telling you some theories and stories today. I have one more to share with you. First, there are some facts you should know. Miss Rockwood made some comments at dinner last night about odd things happening here. I can tell you that she did see some things. Webster Markham had been sneaking into the office every night to use Lizzie's computer without her knowledge."

"Is that why he was arrested?" Locke asked.

"No. When his background was investigated, we found a warrant for his arrest in California. He is being held for extradition pending the outcome of this case."

"What are the charges?" Monty asked.

Wade looked at him for a moment before answering. They would all know when the information was released to the media. "He has been accused of stalking a young girl and child pornography."

No one had anything to say. Wade took the opportunity to share more information. "We have learned that Hawk was here in an attempt to take celebrity photographs and sell them to the highest bidder. He didn't know which rooms were occupied by those people he wanted to exploit. We have evidence that Hawk had been in each of your rooms. He photographed the contents. If you will direct your attention to the big screen, Baker will show you those photos."

Baker started the slide show. Gasps could be heard around the room as each guest recognized their belongings.

"Miss Rockwood saw the lights going on in the guestrooms when Hawk entered the rooms to search," Wade added.

"She wasn't just trying to get attention?"

"No, she wasn't, Monty," Wade assured him.

"Hawk must have found more than he expected to find. His sister said that he phoned her and said he had hit the jackpot so to speak. I believe he left that note for someone and that person met with him. Hawk wanted money to keep quiet about what he'd found. He didn't know that this person had no money. Somehow the camera fell into the pool, and Hawk tried to retrieve it. He or she took the opportunity to hit the man with the rock. The killer felt safe until Miss Rockwood made those comments at dinner. Maybe she had seen or heard something. No one else seemed to take her seriously."

Wade stopped for a moment looking at the faces of the people in the room. Then he continued, "At first we believed that the body in the office was Miss Fletcher. I thought it possible that the killer had made the same mistake. But if these two murders were connected, as I believed them to be, Rachel would have had to be the intended victim."

Wade took a deep breath and surveyed the room. "This is the last story I'll be sharing with you today. Miss Rockwood went downstairs and borrowed a book, this book." he said holding it up. "This media card fell out of the book. Miss Rockwood was curious and wanted to see what was on it. She went into the office. The light had not been turned on so we assume she didn't want to be found. She left the book on the desk, sat down at the computer, and turned it on. She put the card in her mouth and felt with her hands to find the slot to insert the media card. Before she could find it, someone crept up behind her and strangled her with the lamp cord."

Dodson and Lodge took their places quietly. The people listening to Wade didn't notice their movement. Wade nodded at Baker, and he advanced to the next photo.

"This is why Sam Hawk and Rachel Rockwood were killed." Documents and maps were projected onto the screen. Wade waited a moment after the presentation for a reaction from the guilty party. Finally, he asked, "Was this really worth two lives, Monty?"

Dodson and Lodge moved forward and placed their hands on Monty's shoulders. Dodson read him his rights while Lodge prepared to cuff him.

"No! Wait, please!" Monty said pleadingly. "You don't understand. They'll kill me."

"Who will kill you?" Wade asked

"The people I've been working for. You have to help me. Can we make a deal?"

"Tell us what happened, and we'll see what we can do," Wade told him.

"They said we could help each other. They said you have a pilot's license and access to a plane. We have money to pay your debts. They wanted me to pick up a package at the Dallas airport. I thought one time couldn't hurt, and I was coming out ahead on the deal. I didn't realize they had lots of flights in mind."

Baker was taking notes as Monty continued, "The instructions for each flight came by mail on a thumb drive like that one," indicating the picture on the screen. "I thought I was off the hook when I crashed here. Only Rachel knew where I was staying. The last night I was here, she called me and said that she had visitors. She was scared. I was commanded to return or Rachel would suffer. I went home and was told that I still had a package to pick up. The trouble was that I couldn't find the thumb drive. I thought it had to be here somewhere."

"So you came up with a phony movie and brought Markham and Miss Rockwood along," Wade suggested.

"They didn't know it wasn't real. I hoped to find the thumb drive and have a new movie to produce when we left here. Hawk had seen me searching for something. He found the thumb drive in some grass on the edge of the grounds. He plugged it into his laptop and knew it was important to me. He wanted one hundred thousand dollars to keep his mouth shut and his pictures out of the papers. I knocked the camera out of his hands and into the pool. He said he was smarter than that and had the media card in a safe place. I told him that I had to go inside to get my checkbook, trying to buy time to figure something out. I passed the flowerbed and saw the big rocks there. I picked one up and walked back to the pool. He was trying to reach his camera and didn't notice I was there. I hit him hard. He didn't move, so I searched his pockets. I found the thumb drive and the media card and took them."

"Why did you hide the card in that particular book?" Baker asked.

"Rachel had mentioned that she wanted to read it when Ms. Wainrite had finished. The title was easy to remember."

"But why did you kill Rachel?" Lizzie asked, stunned that her friend had killed two people.

"Rachel and I had a big fight. She found the thumb drive and knew I was still working for those people. She said she was going to hand it over to Wade. I took it from her and stuffed it in the inside pocket of the jacket I was wearing. We argued a while longer. Finally, she said she didn't want to fight anymore. She said she was going to find a movie or a book to read. She was downstairs before I realized she had picked my pocket.

I started after her and saw her go into the office. I didn't see a light under the door. I thought she was hiding from me. I remembered the door between Lizzie's room and the office. I went to Lizzie's door and listened. I could hear the shower running, so I went through her room. Rachel was sitting at the computer with her back to me when I opened the office door. She didn't hear me. She was sitting there running her hands over the computer. I thought she was planning to copy the information from the thumb drive.

I don't know what came over me. It was like I was possessed. I kept thinking it was her or me. I picked up the lamp, wrapped the cord around her neck, and pulled as hard as I could.

When her hands fell to her sides, I dropped the lamp on the floor and found the thumb drive in her pocket. I left through the main office door and went back to my room." Monty began to sob, "I saw her reflection in the computer screen. I'll never forget the look in her eyes."

"Did you get it all Baker?" Wade asked.

"I believe so," Baker answered.

Wade nodded at Dodson and Lodge. "Take him in, and tell Maddie to release Megan Hayes."

Dodson and Lodge took Monty to their car and helped him into the backseat. They nodded to the sheriff as they drove away.

Wade returned to the dining room and looked around at the stunned occupants. He noticed Cindy Berkett was standing alone looking at the Fletcher family as they huddled together. He smiled at her and said, "You should tell them who you are. Now is as good a time as any."

"I suppose it is," she said. She took a deep breath and walked toward the Fletcher family. Mr. Locke cleared his throat to get the sheriff's attention.

"I'd like to show you something if you don't mind."

"All right," Wade said.

Locke went upstairs. He returned holding the locked case and wearing the white cotton gloves. He placed the case on a table in the dining room and carefully removed the protective wrapping from the contents. He placed it so that the sheriff could easily see it.

"I've seen these markings before. Lizzie, look at this," Wade called.

Everyone walked over and stared at the object.

"It's lovely," Mrs. Berkett remarked.

"Where did you get this?" Lizzie asked.

The saddlebag bore the initials J.K. and five keys on a key ring. "It's been passed down in my family for generations," Locke told them.

Locke carefully opened the saddlebag and removed an old book. He gently turned the pages and then Wade said, "Well I'll be damned. Here's a hand drawn map of the creek. It shows where those two bodies were buried."

After a few moments he continued. "According to this, the two men that were found here were Frank and Harold Keys," Wade said in astonishment. "How did your family happen upon this?"

"This journal belonged to Joseph Keys," Locke told them. "He was my great grandfather. You'll find all the details about a bank robbery in Willow, Oklahoma, and the events that followed. Frank and Harold Keys were his brothers. After he buried them, he traveled to New Mexico. He changed his name to John Locke and settled down there. It says in the journal that he had hoped to come back and put a marker on their graves. He obviously never managed to do so."

"What does this mark stand for here?" Lizzie asked.

"That was where the money from the bank robbery was buried. I've walked the creek three times since I arrived. I haven't been able to find the landmark indicated there."

"There's no gold on this land," Lois said firmly.

"I know, Mrs. Fletcher. Cash was taken from the bank, not gold. I don't expect to find any of it after all this time, but I would like to find the most likely place it was buried."

"I'm almost ashamed to tell you this," Wade said. "The story is told among my family that my great, great grandfather died out here looking for that money. He bought the land directly across the creek and was looking for the money when he died."

"You're a descendant of Clay Adams?" Lois asked.

"Yes, ma'am."

"It's a small world." Lois said and looked at the map. "The landmarks have changed since this was drawn. This looks to be close to where the bridge is now."

"It was supposed to be thirty paces west from a big tree and across the creek. I haven't been able to find the tree," Locke said.

"The tree in this drawing was struck by lightning when I was a little girl. I can remember it burning for days," Lois told them.

"Do you think you can find where it stood?" Wade asked.

"I think I can," Lois answered. "But I doubt the money would have survived all these years."

"Shall we find out?" Locke asked.

Everyone seemed to agree that they should.

"I'll get some shovels from the shed," James said.

James returned with three shovels. The Fletchers, the sheriff, his deputy, Cindy Berkett, and Mr. Locke made their way to where the old tree once stood. They walked thirty paces toward the west and crossed the creek. They began to dig only three yards from the bridge. The men took turns digging in an area of three square feet.

After digging for some time and finding nothing, Locke said, "Thank you for helping me. I wasn't expecting to find the money. I came here to see if the bodies could be those of my distant uncles and bring this journal to life. As I told the sheriff, there are all kinds of treasure."

"Mr. Locke would you like to follow us into town and meet your long lost uncles," Wade asked already knowing the answer.

"I certainly would. Thank you, Sheriff."

The group slowly walked back to the inn taking the time to unwind before returning to their everyday lives. James and Lois lagged behind the others.

"Mom, do you think the money was ever here?" James whispered.

"Yes, it was once. I don't think they would be happy to know that I allowed them to dig for money that I knew was no longer there. Mr. Locke seems perfectly content. The money didn't belong to him anyway." Lois looked at her son and grinned, "I see no reason to tell them that my grampa found the money when he was a young man."

"Neither do I," James grinned back.

"I hope that this will end the treasure hunting. I'm sure the story will be on the news one evening this week," Lois said.

If it isn't, I'll see what I can do to get it on the news," James told her.

Cindy Berkett decided it was time to return to New York. She arranged for her return flight and a cab. She waved at the Fletchers as the cab drove away.

Baker loaded his equipment into the truck and waited for Wade and Mr. Locke.

"How did the conversation with Mrs. Berkett go Lizzie?" Wade asked.

"It was surprising. I was so sure that I'd recognize her. She said she needed to get away, but I don't understand why she came here. I suppose she needed closure."

"I suppose so." Wade paused a moment and then took Lizzie's hand and said, "Will you have dinner with me tomorrow night?"

"I'd love too," she assured him as she looked into his eyes and felt that familiar feeling run down her spine.

The End

PREVIEW OF DEATH UNDER A FULL MOON

ONE

It was a peaceful mid-September evening in Wilbarger County, Texas. The setting sun painted the sky with ribbons of orange, pink, and gold. The temperature was mild, and the air was still. It was a welcome relief after several days of hot, dry wind.

Brian Flynn shut down the engine on his tractor and sat quietly surveying the land that he and his family loved. The farm house sat near the center on the northern boundary of their two-hundred-acre farm. The land was divided into three fields. He had just finished preparing the east field. It needed to be planted with wheat in the coming week. The center field of alfalfa had given its last crop until spring. The west field was C.R.P. land.

He watched as his ten-year-old son Hunter and his six-year-old daughter Chloe played on the tire swing he had made for them. He smiled as the sound of their laughter floated to his ear. They both had golden hair like their mother, but they had his brown eyes. Kelly opened the back door, waved to him, and called the kids inside.

Brian's stomach grumbled as he started the tractor and drove back to the house.

Inside the house, the Flynn family sat at the kitchen table enjoying their supper. As was their nightly ritual, they discussed the events of the day. Brian listened while the children and Kelly talked. When they had finished, it was his turn.

"I saw some deer tracks near the pond at the edge of the field."

"Can we go see them, Daddy?" Chloe asked.

"We'll go to the pond Saturday."

"Your dad and I will clean up the kitchen. It's time for you two to get your homework done," Kelly told them.

Hunter and Chloe reluctantly obeyed. Homework was the worst part of the day as far as they were concerned.

"You're quiet tonight. What's wrong?" Kelly whispered.

"Nothing," Brian answered, pretending to concentrate on the dirty dishes.

"Brian, look at me," Kelly urged.

Brian looked at his wife silently for a moment. Finally, with a heavy heart, he said, "Jim is going to put his place on the market. He doesn't have any more work for me."

Kelly put her arms around her husband. "What are we going to do?"

"I don't know. It will take a lot of rain to save the farms around here. It may be too late. Water wells are drying up all over this part of the country. Ours isn't producing the amount of water we need to water the crops. If this drought doesn't end soon, we're going to be in serious trouble. I've been trying to decide whether we should plant the wheat next week or take the seed back and put all of our land into C.R.P."

"What's C.R.P., Daddy?"

The couple rolled their eyes and grinned at each other. Chloe was always listening, particularly when the conversations were whispered. Kelly shrugged her shoulders and said, "We may as well tell them."

"It stands for Conservation Reserve Program," Brian told his daughter. "The government will pay us if we put our land in that program for at least ten years. It's supposed to control soil erosion and make a place where wild animals can live."

"Dad, what will we do if you don't farm?" Hunter asked.

"I'll have to find a full time job and drive to town everyday like your mother."

"What about Mr. Jim?"

"Mr. Jim doesn't need my help right now," Brian reluctantly told his son.

The family sat in silence for a few moments pondering the turn their lives were about to take. Finally, Kelly said, "We're going to weigh all of our options before we make such a big decision. Your dad and I will talk about this more later. Finish your homework."

When the homework and evening chores were done, the young couple tucked their children in before going to bed themselves.

"Brian, I'm concerned about the kids. They're too young to have to worry about such things."

"I know. I'm glad they heard it from us rather than someone else. A lot of folks are having the same decisions to make. You know that one of their friends is bound to say something."

"That's true. I guess it's best they know there will probably be some big changes coming. Do you think that we might have to sell out and move to town?"

"I hope not," Brian said as he turned off the light and held his wife close. "We won't even discuss that unless there's no other choice."

Outside the house, the full moon glowed proudly in the evening sky. A small herd of mule deer grazed in what remained of the alfalfa field. A few of them watched the lights of the farm house blink off as its occupants settled down for their nightly dreams. The deer grazed contentedly, unaware that something else watched and waited in the cover provided by the tall native grass of the C.R.P. land.

A young healthy doe slowly wandered away from the herd as she grazed toward the tall grass. Startled, she raised her head and looked at her surroundings. She turned and began to trot back toward the herd. She had taken only a few steps before she broke into a run. Suddenly, she felt a sharp pain in her shoulders. She struggled to free herself from the pain and the weight bearing down on her. The noise she made while battling for her life alarmed the remainder of the herd. They ran in terror as strong jaws delivered the killing bite, breaking the unfortunate doe's neck.

The large animal dragged the deer into the C.R.P. Once satisfied that its catch was safe from other predators, it began to feast on its kill. Using its claws to open the flesh, it ate the heart, lungs, and liver first. When the beast was finally satisfied, it buried what remained and gracefully moved through the native grass, leaving little of its prey behind.

The following morning Brian waved goodbye to his family as they left for the day. He felt good about the decision he and Kelly had made about their future. He was eager to get started. He would find a full-time job and continue to farm during his off hours for the time being. There wouldn't be a lot of farm work to be done until spring. They had decided to plant the wheat as planned. It would be a dry land crop depending on Mother Nature for its needed moisture. In doing so, they hoped they would be able to conserve enough water for irrigating the alfalfa in the spring and summer.

Brian knew it was only a temporary solution. If the drought continued, the water would run out, and the crops would fail. Since neither he nor Kelly could see into the future, they were gambling on one more year to keep their home.

Brian drove into town to see his friend Drew Clifton. Andrew Clifton was vice president at one of the local banks. He had mentioned a job opening the last time they had seen each other.

Brian hoped he still had that opening or at least knew of another one. He had made a ten-thirty appointment for that morning so that he could be sure to see Drew. He arrived ten minutes early and paced restlessly while he waited.

"Brian, how are you?" Drew asked extending his hand to his friend.

"Hi, Drew. Doing okay," he lied. "How are you?"

"Good. Come in. Would you like some coffee?"

"That sounds good. Thank you."

"Sit down. Make yourself comfortable." Drew watched his friend while pouring the coffee. "What brings you into town today?"

Brian took the coffee and sighed. "I suppose you know this isn't a social call."

Drew nodded as he sat down. "I figured as much since you made an appointment. What can I do for you?"

"I need a job, Drew, a full-time job that I can depend on. I thought you might know of someone needing help. My crops weren't good this year, and Jim told me he's going to sell out. I need something other than farming so that I can support my family."

"Are you planning to sell?"

"We decided last night to give it one more year. I've lived on that place all my life. It's the only home I've ever known. I can't stand the thought of selling. Kelly doesn't want to sell either. We're going to try farming on the side and conserving as much water as we can. If things don't improve, we may put it into C.R.P. Selling would be our last resort."

"Do you need a loan? I'd be happy to loan you some money or cosign for a loan."

"Thanks, Drew. I appreciate it; I might have to take you up on that offer later. Right now, what I need is a job. Any job will do as long as the pay is steady."

"There aren't any openings here at the moment. I did hear a

rumor that there has been some turnover at the state hospital. I'll call over there and see what I can find out for you."

Brian waited patiently as Drew turned to his desk phone and dialed a number.

"Paul Randolph, please," Drew said when someone answered. He waited a few minutes before saying, "Paul, this is Drew Clifton. Doing well. How are you? Good, good. Are there any job openings over there? Well, I have a good friend here in my office, and he's looking for a job. You know Brian Flynn don't you?" Drew smiled as he listened and made notes.

"There's a security guard position open. Can you be in Paul Randolph's office at one o'clock this afternoon?" Drew asked Brian as he covered the mouthpiece of the telephone.

Brian nodded, relieved.

"He'll be there. Thank you, Paul."

Drew handed Brian the note paper.

"Thank you, Drew. I really appreciate your help."

"What are friends for? I hope this helps."

The two friends shook hands. Brian left to find some lunch and a place to wait until time for his one o'clock appointment.

After meeting with Paul Randolph, Brian drove to Kelly's office.

"How did it go?" Kelly asked.

"I start orientation Monday morning," Brian answered. "I'm going to be a security guard. It's going to mean working some nights."

"We'll make it work somehow," Kelly assured him.

Brian drove home feeling as if a tremendous weight had been lifted.

***

The sun rose to chase away the dreams of the night. Its light illuminated a landscape which would soon be trimmed with the orange, red, and amber colors of fall. The last Saturday of September promised to be a beautiful day.

Lizzie Fletcher woke to the song of a meadowlark. She lay in bed listening to its song while relishing the comfort of her bed. It was a simple pleasure, one that she seldom had the opportunity to enjoy.

All was quiet at the Paradise Creek Inn. It was the beginning of a temporary lull in a steady and oftentimes booming business. The coming holiday season would keep her family busy into the New Year. Lizzie had made plans to enjoy the downtime.

The Fletcher family owned and operated the inn. As the managing partner, Lizzie lived at the inn and saw to the daily tasks. Her parents and grandmother helped as they were needed.

It was located on the Fletcher family farm in Wilbarger County, Texas. The house had been built by Lizzie's great, great grandfather. It had been her grandmother's suggestion to renovate the old house into an inn.

Looking at the clock, Lizzie decided she had lain in bed long enough. She had things to do before Wade arrived.

She showered and dressed quickly in her favorite jeans and t-shirt. She brushed her shoulder length red hair back from her face and applied a little cosmetic enhancement that showed her vivid blue eyes to the best advantage. Satisfied with her appearance, she went to the kitchen.

Lizzie thought of Wade as she prepared a picnic lunch. She felt a little silly, but she was excited about the day. They had both been so busy that she had not seen him in weeks.

Wade Adams was the Wilbarger County sheriff. They met in April of 2012 when Wade and Dr. Hughes came to her rescue after a storm had practically dropped an injured man on her doorstep.

He was at the inn daily after the bodies were discovered. He had asked her to have dinner with him after the cases were closed. It was hard to believe that it was already nearing the end of 2013 and that they had been seeing each other almost a year-and-a-half.

Lizzie shuddered at the thought of those who had died and who had been responsible for their deaths. It was still hard at times to believe it had all been real instead of a storyline in a movie. She was startled from her reverie when her mother came into the kitchen.

"Something sure smells good in here," Ellen commented.

"Hi, Mama," Lizzie answered as she hugged her mother.

"Fried chicken?"

"Yes, ma'am."

"I guess it's a good thing I didn't plan that for supper tonight. You're planning to be back for supper aren't you?"

"We will. I promise."

"Good. Here's the basket you wanted. I brought this old blanket that Daddy and I always took with us. You can use it if you want."

"That'll be great! Thanks."

"Where are you going for your picnic?"

"I thought I'd take him to the spring."

Ellen smiled wistfully. "We used to love going to the spring. We haven't been in years."

"I hope it's still a nice place to go," Lizzie replied. "I haven't been since I moved home."

"What are you going to do if it isn't?"

"I have a backup plan, but I really want Wade to see the spring."

The phone rang in the office, interrupting the conversation.

"I'll get it."

"Thanks, Mama," Lizzie said as she began packing food into the picnic basket. She went to the pantry for a few finishing touches. As she closed the pantry door, she heard her mother calling her. She hurried back to the kitchen to find Wade smiling down at her and holding three long-stemmed yellow roses tied together with sheer white ribbon.

"Look who I found hanging around out front," Ellen teased.

Lizzie stood smiling up at him for a moment before saying, "Hi, stranger."

"Hi, beautiful. I'm sorry I'm late. I had to stop by the flower shop," he said, handing her the flowers.

"They're my favorite."

"I know," Wade grinned.

"Thank you," she replied as she took the roses and kissed him.

It was a long, passionate kiss. One that said much more than the mere words "I've missed you" could convey. It was the kind of kiss that held a world of meaning to the participants.

Ellen was both pleased and uncomfortable. She felt like an intruder in a very private moment. She wanted to leave, but the young couple blocked her exit. In an attempt to give them some privacy, she began rummaging in the refrigerator. After several minutes, she gave up and loudly cleared her throat.

"Ahem." No response. She tried again, "Ahem." Finally, Ellen said, "You two had better get moving before your lunch gets cold".

The couple broke the kiss and moved aside.

"I'm sorry, Mama. Are you trapped?"

Ellen hurried from the room calling, "You kids have a good time, but don't be late for supper."

"We won't," Wade answered grinning.

"Watch out for the poison oak," she called as she closed the door.

"I'll put these in some water before we go," Lizzie said as she went to the cabinet for a vase.

"Where are we going?"

"Have you ever been to the spring at Rayland?"

"No, I didn't know there was a spring there."

"Daddy used to take me there when I was a kid. I'd like for you to see it. We can have our picnic there and enjoy the afternoon."

"It smells great, and I'm starved."

"We should probably take my jeep. Getting there will involve a little off-roading."

"We can take my truck. I'll provide the transportation since you're providing the meal."

"Okay, but don't say I didn't warn you."

"Where is the spring," he said grinning at her.

"I'll show you. Are you ready?"

Wade picked up the picnic basket. "Lead the way," he said.

Lizzie followed him carrying the blanket. Wade put the picnic supplies in the back seat of his Ford F-150 super crew before helping Lizzie inside.

"Rayland, here we come," he joked as the motor roared to life.

ABOUT THE AUTHOR

Dianne Smithwick-Braden is an avid reader of fiction but mysteries are by far her favorite genre. It seemed only natural that her own novels would be mysteries. Her favorite authors are Agatha Christie, Janet Evanovich, and Clive Cussler. She recently discovered and became a fan of Reavis Wortham.

The Wilbarger County Series is set near Dianne's home town of Vernon, Texas. She was raised on the family farm in the western part of Wilbarger County. She graduated from Vernon High School in 1979.

Dianne currently lives in Amarillo, Texas with her husband, Richard and their dog, Rowdy. She has been a high school science teacher in Amarillo since August of 1990.

There are no hidden agendas or messages in Dianne's work. She writes purely for the entertainment of her readers. She is personally entertained while writing. Her stories are intended to be a temporary escape from the real world.

Dianne's novels are suitable for most audiences. She refuses to write anything that she would be embarrassed for her mother, children, or grandchildren to read.

Please, take a few moments to rate and/or review this book. Dianne would love to know what you think.

Subscribe to Dianne's monthly newsletter at www.diannesmithwick-braden.com.

TITLES BY DIANNE SMITHWICK-BRADEN

Coded for Murder

The Wilbarger County Series

Death on Paradise Creek (Book One)

Death under a Full Moon (Book Two)

Flames of Wilbarger County (Book Three)

Gambling with Murder (Book Four)

Subscribe to Dianne's newsletter at:

www.diannesmithwick-braden.com

Follow Dianne at:

www.facebook.com/smithwickbraden

www.instagram.com/smithwickbraden

twitter.com/smithwickbraden

www.pinterest.com/smithwickbraden

www.goodreads.com

bookbub.com

Made in the USA
Middletown, DE
17 April 2022

64377775R00129